D1602628

Banshee and the Sperm Whale

by Jake Camp

In memory of William "Gatz" Hjortsberg,
who lived on clouds of possibility,
and died on Earth Day.

"Body am I entirely, and nothing more; and soul is only the name of something in the body....The body is a big sagacity, a plurality with one sense, a war and a peace, a flock and a shepherd. An instrument of thy body is also thy little sagacity, my brother, which thou callest 'spirit'—a little instrument and plaything of thy big sagacity....Behind thy thoughts and feelings, my brother, there is a mighty lord, an unknown sage—it is called Self; it dwelleth in thy body, it is thy body. There is more sagacity in thy body than in thy best wisdom."

–Friedrich Nietzsche, *Thus Spoke Zarathustra*

"The dangers of life are infinite, and among them is safety."

–Goethe

Part 1: The Quest of Diver Neurons

Part 2: On the Nature of the Weather System

Part 3: Falling Through the Storm

Part 4: The Intractable Nature of the Sea

Part 5: The Place from which Change is Possible

Part 1: The Quest of Diver Neurons

1 – Martin's Wedding Research

When the pockmarked streets and crooked brown trees of River North started to age like cast iron faces, Martin and Ana knew they must marry. With New Year's past and spring break just around the corner, the swirling winds of commitment began to seep through the walls of their two-story condo, driving through door frames and window wells, making particular suggestions about what it means to insulate their future.

And what did it mean to the thirty-one-year-old Head Chef at Front Range Community College? Besides a simple wedding, a wedding unencumbered by family and friends, by church, by in-laws, by expensive over-the-top things, Martin wanted to get married somewhere exotic, somewhere European, somewhere liberal. A cruise along the Danube with stops in Vienna, Budapest and Belgrade. A trip down the Rhone to Aix-en-Provence. Old-vine Bordeaux, stinky cheese, nude beaches, warm breezes to open up his future wife, wash away her inhibitions.

But Ana wanted an island wedding, so Martin found a website on sunset ceremonies in Kona, Hawaii. Home to the famous green flash, when the sun sinks into the sea, creating a viridescent arc on the horizon, the couple could say "I do" at the shimmering moment. Afterward they could build a fire on the beach and make love on the black sand, while sea turtles slept in the bay, and while the stars and the moon trundled across the sky making white-hot tracers.

Going deeper into the idea of a sunset wedding, Martin stumbled across an older couple who performed ceremonies in Kona. The husband played mandolin. The wife officiated. Neither was religious in a traditional way. Only the native

Hawaiian customs were involved—lava rock, the blending of sands, music, the embracing of mother nature—all of which suited Ana and Martin perfectly.

Maybe too perfectly.

Martin's thoughts grew ambiguous.

Or was it his third beer?

Regardless, the region of his brain that was responsible for embracing routine, convention and lifelong commitment started to light up. Anxious configurations of grey matter formed along his cerebral cortex, along the Weather Region of his brain. Where Sea met Sky, a brown cloudbank had formed near the cingulate gyrus of his frontal lobe. Lightning skewered his prefrontal cortex. Thunder. Hail. A waterspout rotated in the distance. Deep, long, undulating, the entire Weather Region flexed, brooded and began to pulsate.

2 – Marguerite

Martin entered a different website, a non-wedding related website, a website dedicated to swingers, three-way unions and other forms of sexual deviance. In the midst of pure intentions, his brain spinning like a globe, images of the flesh bobbed and weaved along the blistering ether of his Safari operating system. Martin's Apple computer grew hot and began to smoke.

A transgendered beast from Cap Hill.

A couple desiring a third while husband watched.

A woman named Marguerite whose pointy fingers hiked the fluted ridges of her panties like a mountaineer in the Andes.

The website interactive, Martin clicked into Marguerite's profile. Shrouded in blacks, reds and silvers, alluring and dangerous like a boa snake about to choke out its victim, an electrical smell scoured the air. Metallic brown sugar. Gritty. Grinding. Martin rubbed his cursor over Marguerite's eight-ball shaped breasts and turned up the volume on his computer.

"Hello," said Marguerite, her digital voice raspy. "Mmm... that feels good."

"What?" asked Martin. "What feels good?"

"I can feel you touching me. I can feel your cursor on my body."

Conscious that Ana would be out of town on business for two more days, the region of Martin's brain that was responsible for subsuming feelings of sensual pleasure under moral concepts that could guide his day-to-day living became obscured. He plugged in the microphone on his computer and put his headset on. Lightning from the Weather Region of his brain illuminated the Sky.

"Would you and your wife like to play?" asked Marguerite, her voice driving through the headphones.

"I'm not married," said Martin, gazing at a book on the coffee table. *Adrift: Seventy-Six Days Lost at Sea.* "Just looking for some fun."

"Oh, so you are one of those guys."

"Those guys, what do you mean?"

"Like, you want a woman who likes to swing, but you are not a swinger. It's the mentality that you want. I like that."

Marguerite's long chocolate fingers made a deep whirlpool motion in her panties.

Martin's heart pounded like the surf.

"What's your name?" asked Marguerite.

"Ken," said Martin.

"Ken, you don't seem like a Ken to me. But anyway, what are you doing tonight?"

Martin swallowed hard and asked himself what he was doing tonight? How did his innocent Google search for an island wedding lead to this? Why were his shoes tied and the keys to his car dangling from his index finger? How did thoughts about his future wife morph into wanting to fuck a dark mystery?

"Where can we meet?" he asked.

"How about the Hangar Bar on Colfax?"

3 – Diver Neurons

In the arousal center of Martin's brain, just over the farthest reaches of his limbic system, the waterspout that had formed in the Weather Region continued to build. Within minutes the violent funnel transformed into a full-blown EF5-force tornado. Winds whipped across his hypothalamus at 255 mph, swallowing the surrounding cloudbank, creating a mile-wide hole in the surface of the Sea, where a whirlpool twisted and turned like a wounded eel.

But outside the whirlpool, in the deepest parts of the Sea, the water was perfectly calm. And in the calm, where aqueous windows of Martin's present moment framed entranceways to limestone caves that glistened in the night, a group of Diver Neurons were exploring the serpentine tunnels of the ocean blue. With gills that ran along their cellular bodies and fins built for exploration, Diver Neurons were some of the most determined and sincere explorers of the Sea.

But what were the Diver Neurons searching for? Gold? Jewels? Pirate treasures?

No.

Diver Neurons were searching for hot-bodied mermaids. The crown jewels of the Sea, mermaids lived in hard-to-find places. Forbidden places. Places that posed risk. And accepting this risk required a strategy on the part of the Diver Neurons. And strong leadership. Not just any old neuronal cell was capable of leading dangerous missions.

Enter Chuck.

Hefty, battle-tested, brave, strong, mostly intelligent, an overall man among men, Chuck was competent and skilled. Having completed the highest levels of certification for Diver

Neurons, and with twenty-plus-years of experience leading missions to the most treacherous and remote regions of the Sea, Chuck also had a voracious sexual appetite and could sense mermaids a mile away. But where did he get these sensibilities, and why did he have this overall constitution?

It's a question no one wants to face.

Born into adversity and trauma, Chuck's father left his mother when he was eight years old and ran off with a younger woman. And so, raised by a single mother, who at times had to compromise herself to pay the bills, Chuck grew up in a bad part of town, in a dirty part of the Sea, where many creatures came and went in his life. Some of these creatures grew two heads. Others had elongated limbs and spikes along their spine. Still others blended in with the sea floor, only to surface when it was time for a meal.

But as with all great souls, Chuck rose above his circumstances and turned his struggles into strengths. No one really knows why someone can do this, why one neuron will turn down dark alleys and another will not. It's a mystery. Beings in general are a mystery the deeper you go. And Chuck was no exception. Tough, sincere, good-hearted, shaped by adverse circumstances, a man of extraordinary appetites—food, beer, sushi, mermaid pussy—Chuck's desires made him who he was. And they explained why he and the other Diver Neurons would get into trouble from time to time.

Trouble in the ocean brine.

In the Sea of Grey.

In the deepest parts of the ocean blue.

And when this happened, Martin's entire routine, the aims of his life, would suffer. Sometimes it would be depression. Sometimes sleeplessness. Other times a different kind of pain. A pain that would not only hurt himself but others who were close to him.

4 – Hangar Bar

Martin pulled into the Hangar Bar, a dark, seedy dive bar on Colfax Avenue. He opened the door and was greeted by a woman who wore a melanoid leather skirt and four-inch high stiletto heels. Her hair wiry and taut like fine steel wool, Marguerite's appearance was different than it had appeared on the website. Instead of brown, her skin was ghost white. Instead of blue, her eyes burned like a brush fire on the high plains. Instead of tight curves, her body undulated less and sagged more in all places that mattered, north and south.

The bartender poured Marguerite a dirty gin martini. They sat down in a wraparound booth.

"You're hot," said Marguerite, her long fingers rubbing along Martin's inner thigh.

"Thanks," said Martin. "So are you. I noticed your profile said you have an average body. I wouldn't say your body is average at all."

Marguerite bit her lip and laughed as if she'd heard that joke before.

"You're funny."

Martin took a long pull on his beer. "So what is your real name?"

"Marguerite," she said. "Marguerite is my real name."

Martin downed the beer.

"Are we going to do this?" she asked.

"Do what?"

"You know what."

Marguerite's pinky finger made contact with his erection under the table.

"I didn't come here for that," he said.

"Yes, you did."

Martin was about to erupt. His pulse beat hard, but none of it felt within his control. None of it.

"I want you to cum in my mouth," whispered Marguerite in his ear.

"Where can we do this?" said Martin.

"Outside. Just make sure you bring a big tip."

"A tip?"

"I'm not free."

Free.

The word made a sound, but Martin barely heard it. Or if he did, it had transmigrated from one place to the next. But from where?

From *here.*

From hiddenness.

From a world of adventure and unconscious consent.

From the innocent call of a Sea Nymph echoing off the walls of an underwater chamber.

5 – Chuck Finds a Mermaid

"Follow me," bubbled Chuck to the nine billion Diver Neurons that flanked one of Martin's synapse receptor sites.

A mile under the surface of the Sea, unconcerned about the Weather System above, Chuck led the school of Diver Neurons through a cave entrance. Fish of all colors sparkled in the distance. Reds. Pinks. Yellows. Blues. Further in, a mysterious figure appeared. Curvy in the right places, the figure moved in concentric circles in the corner of the cave.

Chuck turned his headlamp on high and motioned for the others to move forward with caution. Testosterone coursing through their veins, the Diver Neurons drew closer to the tight-finned, long-tailed specimen.

"Fish food," Chuck called out, reaching behind his back.

Chuck's second-in-command handed him the mermaid attractant, and he laid a line of pheromone molecules in the water.

"Thanks, Dez."

Open to the chivalry, a mermaid emerged from the shadows. She swam forward. Chuck reached out to touch the mermaid's perky dendrites.

"Easy, Chuck," said Desmond. "Easy. Might be good to ask for her name?"

Chuck looked back to the school of Diver Neurons. Hoping she had friends, they nodded in approval. Chuck placed a bit more pheromone in the water.

"What's your name?" he whispered. "My name is Chuck. I like your tail."

The mermaid turned her head shyly.

"Come on, Chuck," whispered Desmond. "You can do better

than that, man. That's the oldest line in the book."

The nine billion neurons frowned.

But as Chuck prepared to dig deeper into his bag of tricks, the mermaid swam closer.

"My name is Mary. Thank you for noticing my tail."

Chuck could tell that Mary was sweet and understated, which made it more difficult to satisfy his own nature, which is to say a nature framed by the need to have intercourse frequently and freely. While Chuck's moral compass was as tiny as a quark, he did seem to have one hidden in his cellular body.

"Do you wanna go for a walk?" he asked.

This time the Diver Neurons shook their heads from side to side. Usually Chuck had better game than this.

"Ask her if she has any friends," whispered Desmond.

"Do you have any friends?" asked Chuck to Mary.

"Yes, lots of them." Mary paused. "Sure, I would like to go on a walk."

Yes! yelled Chuck to himself, hornier than a bull in a china closet.

Chuck took Mary's hand, and the two lovebirds meandered back to a hidden room in the cave.

6 – Martin and Ana Meet

Martin and Ana first met on a cloudy day at the Front Range Community College cafeteria. Homemade minestrone soup was on the menu, along with smoked turkey sandwiches made with three kinds of cheese. Martin poured the soup into Ana's bowl and complemented her on her mauve vest.

"Your vest kind of matches the weather," he said. "I love overcast days."

Ana smiled as she walked away. Later in the week, she visited the cafeteria again. This time Martin had made lasagna from scratch.

"The food looks amazing," she said. "So much better than your typical cafeteria food." Ana realized she had misspoken. "I mean, it looks really good."

Martin got her drift. "Thank you. It's an old family recipe."

"You made the lasagna yourself?"

"For the most part. I mean, the noodles are not homemade."

Ana's bones tingled. Martin was cute, his mannerisms suggestive. Curly black hair. Brown skin. Penetrating green eyes that suggested a faraway country like Spain or Portugal. "I like your tattoos," she said, noticing black lines under his chef's jacket.

Martin pulled up his sleeve to reveal a strange hybrid creature. "It's an octopus," he said, "with a few other things going on."

"Interesting. Is it half man, half fish?"

"Technically it's a mollusk."

Ana sat down to eat lunch. After she finished, she returned to the kitchen and placed her tray on the counter. "Delicious," she said.

"Glad you liked it," replied Martin, his eyes tracing the contours of her pencil skirt. "It's not every day that I get to violate the culinary expectations of a beautiful woman."

Ana smiled, rewarding him for his efforts. "Maybe we can grab a bite to eat outside of work sometime?"

"Sound good."

"Here's my business card. I usually work until 5:00. Call me. Or feel free to come by my office. I'm in room 342C."

7 – First Date

Their first date was a happy hour at Las Delicious, a Mexican restaurant in downtown Denver. Fresh off a long work week, Martin and Ana shared a basket of chips and salsa, and sipped on top shelf margaritas made with Patron. The conversation jumping from subject to subject, Ana asked Martin what he liked about being a chef, why he started working at FRCC and how long he'd lived in Denver.

"I've been here for ten years now," he said. "I'm originally from Seattle. I guess I took the job at Front Range because it sounded relaxing. Before that, I was an executive chef at a couple high-end chain restaurants, which ended up being stressful. Lots of pressure in the fine dining industry. Lots of long nights." Martin pulled out Ana's business card from his pocket. "What about you? What exactly does the Chair of Academic Excellence do?"

"I'm basically an administrator," said Ana.

"What sort of administrator?"

Ana brushed her black hair away from her pale face. "I do quality control, especially on online courses. Basically, I check to make sure classes have grading rubrics and conform to the school policies. I also respond to student complaints, like when a student disputes a grade or has a problem with his or her professor."

"Sounds interesting."

"I guess it is, but I do wish I could be a little more creative in my job. There's a lot of politics and bureaucracy, if you know what I mean."

Martin did not know what Ana meant, but was intrigued.

"So, are you originally from Colorado?" he asked.

"Yep, Colorado native."

Ana raised a shrimp fajita to her mouth, sealing in the juices with her lips.

"Yum, this is good."

"I'm glad you like it."

Martin sipped his margarita and noticed the heaviness of the glass when he set it down. Solid. Stable. Not inclined to tip over. Much like Ana, he speculated. Feeling the salt and lime slide down his throat, Martin felt a powerful attraction to her. This was the kind of woman he wanted, he thought. Someone different from him. Someone together. Someone principled. No wind. No lightning strikes in all directions. No ambiguous clouds on the horizon. Only clear skies with moderate precipitation.

8 – The Wedding

On the day of their wedding, the rain started early. Buckets of acidic water spewed from the sky. The biggest Hawaiian storm in fifty years, the downpour was considered a positive omen, an indication of abundance. A child would surely be in their future. But instead of feeling excited, Martin and Ana felt gloomy and fearful, their love darkened by the deluge of the day. Wind blew. The streets of Kona flooded. Karmic worry and superstition hung in the air.

But only an hour before the wedding, the rain stopped, and Punalu'u Beach was quiet. A rainbow formed on the bay; storm petrels swooped across the sky. And the husband and wife who were officiating the wedding made Martin and Ana feel calm, like it was just another day in paradise. Just another trip to eternity.

"*E Hoomau Maua Kealoha.* May your love last forever," said the wife, who poured the white, green and black sands into a triangular vase. "Each color of sand symbolizes a unique part of marriage," she continued. "The white represents purity. The green represents the boundless, overflowing qualities of marriage. While the black sand points to the physical realm where each person is committed to spending intimate moments with only each other. Once the jar is sealed, a pattern has been created unlike any other that has ever existed."

In anticipation of the big moment, Martin squeezed Ana's hand at the center of a clementine sun beam and mouthed the words "I love you." *Aloha au ia 'oe.* Three colors of sand. Two souls carried by sea and shore. *Male ana e pili mai aloha kaua.* We two will cling to love in marriage. The husband played the final notes of *Ke Kali Nei Nu* on his mandolin, and everyone took their places.

"Martin, do you take Ana to be your lawful wedded wife? Do you promise to support her in all her dreams and aspirations, to always cherish her presence and never let your eyes close for the night with anger in your heart?"

"I do."

"Ana, do you take Martin to be your lawful wedded husband? Do you promise to support him in all his dreams and aspirations, to always cherish his presence and never let your eyes close for the night with anger in your heart?"

"I do."

The woman placed yellow leis around their necks.

"By the authority granted to me by the state of Hawaii, it is with great pleasure that I now pronounce you husband and wife. You may now kiss the bride. *Honi ka wa'ha.*"

Martin wrapped his arms around Ana. Slow, tender, their bodies merged together for the official kiss, just as the sun left the sea creating the famed emerald-green flash. When the ceremony finished, both breathed a sigh of relief; tension escaped their chests; they were finally here. *Here.* At that perfect destination in life where anything is possible, everything is meant to be.

But as with all great stories, there is a limit to their narrative structure, a price to pay for being released into the world. And though our stories sustain and inspire, they also surprise us, or hold us back, or put us in places we do not know how to get out of—places that bely their original purpose and leave us in the dark about what to do when the sun goes down.

9 – Sexual Problems

The grey sheets of the bed seemed stiff, the white curtains almost too white. Ana rolled over and rubbed Martin's stomach.

"It's okay, babe. It happens to everyone."

Ana touched Martin's inner thigh.

"Do you want me to help?"

She kissed his chest, slowly moving downward.

Martin felt too cerebral, like there was too much talking, too much back-and-forth. How would he let Ana know?

"Talking less would help. Of course, it's not you," he said. "I'm just stressed, and for some reason talking makes me think too much."

"Just relax. It's no big deal," said Ana.

But of course it was a big deal. And the more they discussed it, the bigger deal it became. A man will always find this problematic, want to run from it, find anything possible to make himself feel like more of a man. And when this happens in marriage, there's a unique weight to the situation. When will the sun rise?

"It's totally normal," said Ana. "Happens to a lot of men."

Martin's frustration grew.

"Let's move on, stop talking about it. Let's just be."

Ana withdrew her hand from Martin's chest. "I'm just trying to help. You know I like conversation when we make love."

"But can we ever talk dirty?" asked Martin.

"You know how that makes me feel."

"You can see how I feel as well."

"What do you think we should do?"

"Nothing," quipped Martin. "We're going to do nothing. Or maybe just have a few drinks more often. Maybe we need to relax, have a little fun and quit thinking so much."

Martin turned over, laid on his back and watched the ceiling fan twirl. An ache over his eyes, he could feel the stress expand. This was not the first time he'd experienced sexual problems with Ana. In fact, it had become a theme. He couldn't find a free and relaxed state. And watching porn likely didn't help. Maybe the articles were right. Maybe porn really does rewire a man's brain. Or maybe it doesn't rewire, but create. New images. New archetypes that demand a man's full attention, pulling him into a deeper unconscious narrative.

Where the thrill of the hunt intensifies.

And a dark Temptress appears.

Salty. Powerful. Alluring. Her presence overwhelming, danger fully real.

10 – Banshee

At a craggy rock outcropping on Martin's parietal lobe, where breaking waves threatened to damage several Diver Neurons who were studying estrus patterns, a shadowy figure swished its tail. Although the figure's nature was unclear, it appeared she had plump breasts and hips that went on for days. With womanly features like these, everyone was excited. But the feminine sea creature edged toward the danger zone where the breakers met the jagged rocks below the surface of the Sea.

Seeing both the allure and risk of the situation, Chuck turned to a young diver in training named Zeke.

"We need to get deep quick so we can assess the situation," he said. "See those white bubbles? They mean the Sea is in a bad mood and could throw us into the rocks. One wrong move and we're dead."

The seventeen-year-old inner-city kid who had lost his father in a drive-by shooting looked at Chuck in a skeptical manner.

"We done gone deep for the last three weeks," said Zeke, clearly frustrated.

Chuck wiped his pheromone detector with his glove and gazed into Zeke's eyes. Knowing Zeke was at the early phase of his sexual maturity, Chuck showed compassion.

"I know we've had a dry spell, but you need to be patient, watch and learn."

Zeke shook his head. "Watch and learn," he mumbled under his breath. "I be watching and learning to my grave."

The shadowy figure swished its tail again, and Chuck placed a dendrite around Zeke.

"Here's what we're gonna do," he said, trying to find those experiential factors in Zeke that could teach him sound prudential reasoning. "We're going to circle back in the opposite direction, and we're going to approach her from the other side, where the water is calm and where there's caves. These caves will protect us from the waves so we can better survey the situation."

Many of the Diver Neurons watched Chuck's interaction with Zeke closely and wanted to know why Chuck felt the need to explain himself to this high-school dropout with stints in juvie for unruly behavior. Some even noted that Chuck was being inconsistent for accepting Zeke into the expedition when there were more qualified divers. But the fact is Chuck rooted for underdogs and even saw a little of himself in Zeke. On top of that, Chuck had a mentorship program in place where Desmond served as Zeke's big brother.

Chuck motioned for the Diver Neurons to follow his lead.

"Be patient," he whispered to Zeke. "I realize it's tempting to try to catch this mermaid straight away, but if we set the hook too early, she'll be gone. Likewise, if we bull rush her, we could go crashing into the rocks."

Zeke thought Chuck was acting like a drama queen. "Chuck done lost his edge, man. He acting like a little bitch," he whispered to another Diver Neuron in training.

The shadowy figure began to speak.

"Hello," she said in the language of Echolocation.

"Hello," Chuck responded, a fluent speaker of both English and Echolocation.

"I like your big backpack," she said.

"Thank you," responded Chuck, sensing double meaning. "Those are supplies for the expedition, lunch and whatnot."

Billions of Diver Neurons fixated on the voice and wondered when Chuck would make a move.

"Let's do this," said Zeke, who did not speak Echolocation and could only hear wavy sounds.

"Quiet down," said Chuck. "This might not be a mermaid."

The cocksure seventeen-year-old continued to question Chuck's leadership. "Shit makes no sense."

Chuck squared up to Zeke, put a dendrite finger in his chest. "You are risking the safety of the entire operation. Now, get to the back of the line."

Zeke shook his head from side to side. "All right, man. I'm outta here." Several of the younger neurons, many fatherless like Zeke, began to follow him. Over the last six months, since Zeke had joined the Diver Neurons, he had gained quite a following. Charismatic, precocious, strong, built like a brick shithouse, Zeke inspired many to wonder if he should be second in charge.

"Has Chuck turned gay on us?" he asked a group of Diver Neurons. "Here we got this damn big booty stripper, and Chuck wants us to swim the other direction? Where his mind at, man? We ain't had no mermaid cooch for weeks. Chuck needs to pull the trigger on this shit."

Tensions were high. Diver Neurons vibrated intensely. A wall of them began to form, pushing on Chuck's back.

Chuck asked for the shadow figure's name.

"Banshee," the shadow said, her echolocation pattern fracturing like veins.

Banshee, said Chuck to himself, watching her legs pull apart, revealing a juicy center. *Weird name.*

The force behind Chuck continued to build, and fending off the Diver Neurons grew increasingly difficult. Meanwhile, in the outside world above the Sea, thunder boomed, giving the entire ocean a chaotic and untrustworthy feel. Chuck's nerves were on high alert.

11 – Text Messages

The alarm clock did not go off in time. Ana hopped out of bed. Late for work, she turned on the shower and ran shampoo through her hair. Drying herself off, she stumbled into the kitchen to brew a pot of coffee. The coffee dripped from the machine like crude oil. That was the essence of the morning. Nothing seemed right. Time. Space. Causality. Ana tripped over a pile of laundry at the foot of the bed. Martin's phone sat on the dresser. She picked it up.

7:55.

A series of texts smattered the screen.

"Where are you at?" said one.

"I'm throbbing," said another.

The texts were dated from yesterday when Ana was still at work. Others were time-stamped to later in the evening when she was sleeping. She couldn't help herself. Ana scanned the messages and clicked deep into his phone to the long stream of texts.

"What are you doing?" said one.

"How did you get my number?" Martin texted back.

"I saved it in my phone."

Ana's eyes could not stop.

"I'm at work, finishing up," replied Martin.

"Finishing up? Wanna go out for a drink after?"

Ana continued to scroll through the messages. There were dozens, including her own.

"Hey, what's up?" asked Ana in one text. "Just seeing what you wanted to do for dinner."

"Oh, I haven't really thought about it yet."

A text from Marguerite. "I'm bored."

A text from Ana. "It looks like this meeting is going to run a little long today. I think I'll be home late."

From Marguerite. "Let's meet at the City Park Grill for dinner and appetizers."

From Ana. "Can you save me some leftovers?"

Ana dropped the phone and walked over to the bed where Martin slept. She leaned over and began to shake him.

"Wake up!" she said. "Wake up! What are these?" She placed the phone in front of his nose. "What are these messages on your phone?"

Martin sat up, took a drink of water, tried to sort out the difference between fact and fiction.

"Babe, nothing is going on. It's just a conversation. I was just texting."

Ana began to cry.

"I'm late and I need to get to work now. But we need to talk. We need to have a serious talk."

Ana stomped out of the bedroom and slammed the door. Dust fell from the overhead fan. Martin's phone buzzed. Another text from Marguerite. 8:15 in the morning and she was still prowling. Thank God Ana didn't see it.

Martin didn't respond to the text, but a subtle kind of horniness lingered over his thoughts. He tossed his phone on the mattress, laid back on the pillows and closed his eyes. Martin felt high. High like he was an amateur flier, amateur in the ways of marriage, in his ability to control his own flight. Although he loved Ana deeply, he felt fractured, out of touch with certain parts of himself. As if a mental barrier had been built, an *invisible partition* of the psyche made of materials he did not choose, Martin's emotions were skewed, his perspectives on value and meaning divided into two different worlds. Two different modes of existence.

Water and Air.

Sea and Sky.

Stress cracks and punctures that ran along the floor of the partition.

12 – Angel Neurons

In the moral center of Martin's brain, near the steepest part of his prefrontal cortex, where the Storm threatened to unleash softball-size hail on his foreseeable future, Martin's capacity to think wisely was compromised, his ability to synthesize love with self-gratification was but a small ray of light compared to the dense cloud cover directly overhead. Being at the mercy of the Storm, a storm that was often present in his day-to-day living, Martin's only hope was to stumble upon a catalyst, something to cut through the swirling winds, open up new pathways to the meteorological center of the self.

Enter that catalyst: Angel Neurons, specifically Nate.

"Lord, let us eat this meal with peace and joy. Let us feel God's hand guide the fork to our mouths," said Nate's father, Pastor Samuel.

Nate burped.

"Please excuse yourself, Nathaniel," replied Pastor Samuel.

Nate did not like the name Nathaniel. "I'm sorry, Dad, excuse me. I just don't understand why we have to say the same thing before each meal," said the twenty-year-old neuron.

Angel Neurons loved saying grace before their evening meal. They found the tradition suggested hope for their futures and placed them in a hypothetical union with the divine, which settled their minds. The tradition did not settle Nate's mind, which frustrated his father.

"Son, this tradition has sustained a community of believers since the beginning of time. Giving thanks to the Lord for our meal is the least we can do."

Nate surveyed the meat on his plate, which made him nauseous. While the rest of the Angel Neurons ate the cow like cows, Nate picked at his food, desiring a purely vegetarian meal. In general, Nate liked eating vegetables, minus the occasional splurge in chicken when he felt the need for protein. Over the years, Pastor Samuel had grown increasingly frustrated with his son's eating habits. "What type of kid doesn't like a good steak?" he often asked himself.

Nate looked down at his feet where the clear Plexiglas floor gave way to the Storm below.

"Dad, but how do we know people aren't starving in the rest of the world?"

The Storm twirled violently.

"And not only that, I have been reading books on vegetarianism. These books say we could feed the world's population if we quit eating meat. And, to be honest, a lot of them suggest religion is a part of the problem, as religion encourages us to view animals as put here for our use."

Pastor Samuel shook his head. Having long-ago tried to ignore his son's radical nature, a nature that revealed itself at a young age, he began to wonder if there was something greater inside his son. Maybe that something was spiritual in nature, maybe non-spiritual; he couldn't tell. Pastor Samuel could only sense that Nate was different from the rest of the Angel Neurons. And in truth, he could sense a certain power inside his son.

Nate pushed aside his steak and studied the Storm below his feet.

"Son, you know it probably isn't a good idea to look too far into the Storm."

Nate thought about Nietzsche.

"Dad, I don't want this steak tonight. Do you mind if I just have another baked potato and a salad?"

Pastor Samuel nodded in concern. Too many signs now pointed to the rough road ahead of Nate, a road he feared would lead his son to dark places. Having only read about Angel Neurons with this temperament, Pastor Samuel worried that his son's life journey would be painful and difficult.

A look of entanglement in his eyes, a reflection of the unknown, Nate continued to stare through the Plexiglas floor into the Storm, while his father wondered why certain neurons are made this way. Why would God allow this? Why are some disposed to look into the abyss? Is it sin? Recklessness? A propensity to hurt one's self? Why do some neurons want to embark on difficult journeys to the very tallest mountains in the world? And why are the tallest mountains in the world under the Sea?

Part 2: On the Nature of the Weather System

13 – Doctor Barrantine

Ana and Martin walked through low-hanging mist to Dr. Barrantine's office. Located a mile from their house in River North, where breweries and restaurants popped up like earthworms in the rain, two statues of Greek figures marked the entranceway to an old Victorian mansion. Opening the door, they followed a spiral staircase to the third floor where a dark brown mahogany door read: DR. BARRATINE, EXPERIMENTAL PHILOSOPHICAL COUNSELOR.

Ana knocked gingerly. A lanky figure wearing a navy-blue corduroy sports jacket and rimless glasses greeted them.

"Please come in and make yourselves comfortable," said Barrantine.

Ana took off her scarf and sat down on the tweed couch. "I love this building."

"Thank you; late 1800s architecture, influenced by the Romanesque style of Henry Hobson Richardson. I have always found it quite provocative." Barrantine raised a cup of oolong tea to his mouth. "So, tell me, what brings you here today?"

"We're here for marriage counseling," said Ana, softly. "We saw your ad in the Westword and thought your practice sounded interesting. My husband, Martin, took a few community college philosophy courses over the years and enjoyed them."

"Very good," said Barrantine. "I used to teach at the community college level years ago. A gratifying experience to be sure. And I'm glad you noticed that this is not your standard practice. You'd be surprised how many couples come here seeking traditional therapy." Barrantine leaned back in his chair. "I imagine you'd both like to know more about my background?"

"Sure," said Ana.

"So, to get the academic part out of the way, I have a doc-torate in philosophical therapy with a special emphasis in the philosophy of technology and the metaphysics of language. I also have a modest background in personal identity theory." Barrantine took another drink of tea, cleared his throat. "But that probably doesn't tell you much. Basically, I was trained as an analytic philosopher, and one of the starting points of the analytic tradition is a careful attention to language. Because words take root in the brain, because they are the bearers of our feelings and template to our psyches, I have always found it critical to explore new ways of communicating with each other."

Barrantine turned his head to the corner of the room. A box rested on a pedestal. "And this sometimes gives rise to ex-perimental methods."

"Experimental?" asked Martin.

"Yes, for years, I followed a Socratic model of philosophi-cal counseling, in which I relied on asking questions about the self—Who am I? What is my mind? What type of values do I hold? How do my culture, upbringing and education contrib-ute to my sense of self? That kind of thing. And while I still find this method useful, I have come to believe that questions do not penetrate the unconscious logic of our grey matter deeply enough. Because the human person is too varied, too difficult to completely crack, unknowable in certain respects, inde-terminate in others, I believe each relationship is unique and poses its own set of challenges. Hence the need for external modalities."

Again, Barrantine eyed the black box in the corner of the room.

"To give a concrete example, recently I saw a couple who were musicians, and there was a point at which the typical cognitive and philosophical strategies simply failed, as we had plumbed the depths of verbal communication as far as we could. In the end, we turned to music, where the couple picked up instruments and began writing and performing songs here in the office. Even though they had the same occupation, they had never fully connected to each other's passions in an intrinsic way."

"Interesting," said Martin.

"So, do you believe this could be beneficial?" asked Barrantine. "Do you believe it would be helpful to approach your relationship in less orthodox ways?"

Martin and Ana studied the curious decor in Barrantine's office. A sculpture made of spoons and forks. A worry doll from Africa. Black and white photos of Monk and Mingus, Kandinsky and Pollock, Joyce, Mailer, and others covered the walls. Although nervous, Martin and Ana nodded their heads. "Yes."

14 – Letting Down

Barrantine walked over to his electric teapot and poured himself a second cup of tea. He sat down, slid open his drawer and laid out a set of colored pencils. "Let's start from the beginning. What brought you together as a couple? How did you meet?"

Ana spoke up.

"We met at work, actually, at Front Range Community College in Westminster. I am an administrator there. Martin is the kitchen manager. We just kept seeing each other, and one day we decided to go out."

Martin rubbed Ana's shoulders.

"That's a nice story," said Barrantine, who began outlining a landscape in his notebook. "Of course, these days, couples usually meet through online dating. Now, how long have you known each other? How long have you been married?"

"We've been dating for seven years, married for two months."

"Two months. Not long. What are your interests? How do you enjoy spending your time?"

"We both love dining out and going to different cultural events like museums, art galleries, movies, that kind of thing," said Ana. "Last weekend we rewatched the whole *Matrix* series."

"Wonderful," said Barrantine. "I'm a big fan of *The Matrix* myself, and I believe its depth is underappreciated. People are often unaware that it functions as a kind of allegory—what we can know versus what we perceive. What is real versus what is fake. What shackles our minds versus opens our hearts."

Martin and Ana listened closely.

"What else?" continued Barrantine. "Martin, what types of activities would you add to the list?"

"We both like to hike."

"Yes, good. Do you hike regularly?"

"Not as much as we used to."

"And what do you enjoy about hiking?"

"The freedom of it, for one," said Martin. "Just being away from the city. I feel like Ana is more relaxed. I don't believe we've ever had an argument when we hiked."

Barrantine drew a set of mountains, then changed pencils from brown to red.

"And when you are not hiking, what do you argue about?"

"Oh, different issues," said Martin, smirking. "Household duties is a big one."

Ana jumped in. "Martin does a lot of the cooking. I do most of the other stuff."

"I see," said Barrantine. "So there are different expectations in terms of how you would like to keep and maintain the house, different perspectives on the division of labor. What else causes issues?"

Ana nudged Martin.

"Do you want to tell him?"

"Tell him what?"

"About the texting?"

Martin rolled his eyes.

"Yeah, so we had this situation where I was texting someone, just for fun, and Ana was reading my texts."

"I accidently stumbled across them when your phone buzzed."

Martin's jaw tightened. "I was just messing around. I made a mistake, which I apologized for."

The tone of Barrantine's sketches changed. Fast motions.

Crosshatching lines. Letters, numbers, symbols. A computer keyboard at the base of a mountain. "I didn't think we would get to this today, yet how often do you use technology in general, like computers, tablets and gaming systems? How frequently do you get on Facebook, Instagram, Twitter and the like? I noticed you've both checked your phones several times since you've been here."

Ana covered her iPhone with her purse. "I guess we use our cell phones a lot. I spend a good part of my work day on a computer."

"And Martin?"

"Not as much. I don't use my computer at all when I'm at work."

Barrantine drew the Apple computer symbol over the mountains. "Apart from the texting episode, has technology contributed to your difficulties in your marriage?"

"Actually," said Martin, "I think it comes into play quite a bit."

"Can you give me an example?"

"Ana spends a ton of time on her computer, even at home. So, like last Friday night, we got in an argument over it. I guess we were in different head spaces."

Ana gave Martin a long stare. "I don't like to use alcohol to decompress. I wasn't in the mood to get drunk."

"I wasn't drunk," said Martin, running his hand across his jawline. "I had a few beers."

"Your beers are high in alcohol."

"See, this is part of the problem. I feel like I am being monitored, and I can't let down."

Barrantine shaded in the Apple logo with orange, then sketched a few light clouds. He closed his notebook, lifted his head.

"Martin, I'd like to get a better sense for this dynamic, in terms of what it means for you to let down. Are you referring to letting down from work or your private life? Please try and paint the picture. What does it feel like for you to relax on a Friday night? What are you hoping to experience when you do let down? What are your needs, wants and motivations? Please try to describe your feelings in the clearest way possible. When you reflect on what you want to do on the weekend, what comes to mind?"

15 – Diver Neurons Grow Horny

Chuck and the rest of the Diver Neurons swam in a long arc around Banshee. Although the swim to safety took longer than anticipated, the Diver Neurons found a cave that gave them a clear line of sight. "Come closer," said Banshee in Echolocation, her breasts swaying back and forth in the bubbles, ass shaking side to side like a stripper on a pole.

The loins of nine billion Diver Neurons oscillated intensely.

"Are you a mermaid?" asked Chuck, checking his depth finder.

"Uhhh...yes, I'm a mermaid," said Banshee, "and I am wet."

The sexual tension was as thick as a field of jellyfish, and everyone's libidos raged out of control. Thankfully, Chuck still had a certain restraint from his two-plus decades of experience, when on more than a few occasions, he had encountered duplicitous mermaids of all varieties. Women who wanted to get pregnant for the sake of a paycheck, for example. Or genetically crazy sluts in search of revenge sex. Who knows if a husband might be lurking behind a rock?

Desmond swam around nervously. Although he wanted to dip his wick as much as the next guy, something made him hesitant. Looking to the back of the line, he could see a group of Diver Neurons moving forward with reckless intent.

Desmond nudged Chuck. "What do you think, boss? This doesn't feel right. I wonder if we should pull up stakes on this Banshee chick. I'm not sure she's worth the risk."

Chuck surveyed the encroaching group of Diver Neurons. "I hear you, Dezzy, but it might be too late to retreat. Let's hold off for a minute. We leave now, and we risk a revolt, or the entire expedition could lose confidence, which could set us back for months. What we need to do is figure out who this woman is. We need her to reveal herself. And we need the ocean to calm down before we make our next move."

"Do you think I should make an announcement," asked Desmond, "to let everyone know they need to be patient?"

Chuck looked back again and noticed punches being thrown. Several Diver Neurons had been tossed from the line completely. Blood feathered out into the water.

"It's too late, Dez. Let's just wait and see what happens."

16 – Fridays

Martin and Ana stepped into Barrantine's office for their second session. They examined the room. The furniture had been rearranged. The desk was swapped out for the couch, his bookshelf moved from one side of the room to the other. A spider plant dangled over the table where the black box sat. Behind it, a cracked painting of Ludwig Wittgenstein nestled against the wall.

"Last week we spoke about my practice," said Barrantine, twizzling his beard. "We discussed what brought you here, and we ended up focusing on what it means for you, Martin, to let down. So, I'm curious, how did this most recent Friday go?"

"Better," said Martin. "We hung out, relaxed, played a game of Scrabble. Maybe the counseling had an effect, you know?"

"Yes, the observer affects the observed. It's a truth that applies to many areas of our lives. Apart from the counseling, was anything different?"

Ana spoke up. "We made a point of keeping the house clean, so when we got home, there wasn't a ton of work to do."

"Very good, and I can appreciate what you are saying. To clarify, Ana, would you say you are an orderly person?"

"On the whole, yes."

"And Martin, where do you fit on the scale of orderliness?'"

"I'm on the far side of the scale. Ha, ha."

"And has this always been a dynamic in your relationship?"

"I guess," said Ana, "but over time, I think we both realized that all this work has to get done. It's not like I love cleaning bathrooms and balancing our checkbook every month. I do it because we need to."

Martin shrugged his shoulders. "Right, but there's also a

time when we need to let go of the house. And here's the thing. I feel like I was honest with you about who I am. We discussed this before we started dating seriously."

"I guess I'm guilty of not fully satisfying my contractual obligation," said Ana, sarcastically. "But people often have these realizations after they are married. They realize what does and doesn't work. And these disagreements are affecting several areas of our life."

"Such as?" asked Barrantine. "Can you elaborate?"

Ana crossed her arms.

"It's affecting our intimacy. Basically, Martin is not always so interested. And I feel like we don't always have the right connection."

"Thank you for your honesty here, Ana. How long have these challenges with intimacy been going on for?"

"Since we got married, I'd say, or possibly a few months before." Ana's eyebrows furled. "And then you throw in the fact that you were texting another woman. How do you think that makes me feel?"

"Babe, it's not like I don't want things to be better. But the house will never be in the perfect state. There will always be shit to do. I guess I just wonder why we can't accept the fact that the house will be messy, especially on Friday nights."

Barrantine listened closely to the exchange.

"Unfortunately, our time is up. But I thought our conversation was quite fruitful. Now, just to confirm, since next Monday is Ana's birthday, we are meeting two weeks from now. After next session, I would like to meet with each of you individually."

17 – Ana's Birthday

Martin's phone vibrated in his shirt pocket as he cut onions to place in the marinade for Ana's birthday dinner. He reached up, pinched the phone with two fingers and proceeded to set the dinner table. Martin placed a red tablecloth down, along with a bottle of Seven Deadly Sins Zinfandel in the center. Hoping the wine would be a good conversation starter, he swirled the luscious magenta liquid into a decanter and walked back to the kitchen. A pile of fresh Provencal spices sat on the cutting board. He put the spices in a Ziploc bag along with olive oil, red wine, onions, salt, pepper and two perfectly cut flatiron steaks.

His phone buzzed again. A text from Marguerite: "I'm here. LOL."

"Where?" Martin typed.

"I could be anywhere. Your place?"

Martin wandered over to the stereo and hit random. Miles Davis' *Bitches Brew* started playing. He sat down on the couch, stared at his phone in disbelief. Despite the counseling, why did he continue to tempt himself with the texts? Like, really. What's the point? It's not like he gave two shits about Marguerite.

Martin took a blast from his pocket vaporizer.

"My wife is coming home soon," he typed.

"She can join. LOL."

"I thought you were going to stop texting me."

"Why don't you block my number if you don't want to talk?"

That *was* the question. Why didn't he block her number?

Martin felt tingly, his mind heavy, relaxed, as if he were detaching from the everyday world.

The door flung open. Ana walked in. Fatigued, drained from work, she dropped her bag on the couch. The CD switched to Coltrane. *Interstellar Space* pumped through the speakers. A shotgun sax scattered in different directions. The natural chaos within. Had Coltrane understood the Storm better than anyone who had ever existed? Martin knew Ana hated *Interstellar Space*, found it schizophrenic, destabilizing, a far cry from romantic. What was he thinking?

Ana's face trended downward to the vaporizer pen on the coffee table. *Are we not in counseling? Is this not my birthday? Do you not realize I just got home from a stressful day of work? What do you not understand about this?*

"Happy Birthday," said Martin, placing his phone in his pocket. "What's wrong?" he asked, slow to realize this was never a good question to ask when something *was* wrong.

"It's been a rough day."

Another rough day, Martin said to himself, his phone buzzing again.

"I'm sorry, babe. Can I make you a drink?" Perhaps he could funnel his horniness for Marguerite into a slow burn for Ana?

"I have a headache. Let me take an aspirin. Maybe in a bit."

Martin stood up and gave Ana a hug. "Let me know."

Ana walked away.

Martin began typing a message to Marguerite.

"I can't talk now. But I am horny," he said. "Very horny."

Hello? Was his mouth broken? A sock stuck in the hinges? Did he lose control of his fingers? Did Coltrane threaten to destroy all cognitive thought? Martin poured a glass of wine, fired up the grill.

Ana came out of the bathroom and seemed more relaxed.

"I'll take a drink now."

"A salty dog?"

"Sounds good."

Now we're talking.

Martin squeezed the grapefruit juice into a shaker and poured the vodka in. He reached down and shut his phone off. The texts could wait, or maybe he could delete them entirely. Baby steps. Change does not happen overnight. Even if there were clouds in the distance, or a little rotation, possibly a bit of hail, Martin could feel himself want to resist the dark urges.

He could feel a desire to understand the north-south orientation inside himself.

The partition that had been built as a young boy running through the streets of Seattle at all hours of the night. Honking noises. Steam. Red light. Green light. *Chasing the Trane.* Mom was busy cleaning houses, or maybe she was at home, bedroom shaking, headboard slamming, screaming, heating up, howling at the moon.

No one ever modelled true goodness in Martin's life. No one pointed out badness. No one lived in the middle ground. The in-between. The normal. The place where most people dwell. There were no role models in Martin's life. No heroes. No young adult archetypes who could help show him the way.

18 – Nate Studies the Storm

The Angel Neurons' home shook violently. Every once in a while, the Storm below would rattle the entire place, and the whole community of Angel Neurons would hunker down in their rooms for the night, heads tucked under their covers like they were nesting. When the Storm grew this strong, everyone was on edge, worried that the precipitation would reach the inside of their home as it had years earlier, when tiny rivulets of water dripped down the walls, making unsettling spider patterns.

Not knowing what any of this meant and being prone to superstition, Angel Neurons relied on prayer and a bit of inductive reasoning to try and understand what they had done in the past to warrant the precipitation. Was it sin? Retribution? Cosmic chaos? Although they never did get answers to these questions, they assumed God was trying to keep them humble by sending them a stern but gracious warning about who was in charge.

Nate stared long and hard through the Plexiglas to the cumulonimbus clouds swirling below. A bowl of spirulina noodles in his hand, he raised a spoonful to his mouth and let the intensity of the Storm settle into his fibers. Calm was the dominant feeling. Like he was in the presence of a greater energy. Not God-like greater, but mystery itself. The essence of life. A journey without a transcendental roadmap. Of course, speculations about the Creator were always there for the taking, but for Nate these answers felt canned, too simple, as if he had a higher calling that was incompatible with religious faith.

Nate pressed the binoculars to his face and gazed into the center of the Storm. What *really* was below, he wondered? Below the Plexiglas, the Clouds, the Storm, the Sky itself? Why did it grow dark on some days while settling down on others? Why did it strike fear into the hearts of the Angel Neurons? Was it worry, caution, insecurity? Something learned? Something genetic? Or maybe they were the smart ones, and Nate's obsession with the Storm was rooted in a kind of starry-eyed immaturity?

19 – Upbringing

A winter storm fell in the Denver metro area, dropping six inches of snow. Late for their appointment with Dr. Barrantine, Martin and Ana jumped in the car and began driving. The roads were treacherous. Heavy, wet snow crystals formed a thick layer of ice on the asphalt. Martin fishtailed as he pulled onto Brighton.

"Slow down," said Ana.

Martin responded with harsh words. A theatrical aspect to the conversation, they began arguing, playing to the therapy session. Something fresh and juicy to talk about. A self-fulfilling prophecy. Less censored than usual, Martin criticized Ana for being uptight. He criticized her for other things. His criticisms were personal.

When they arrived at Barrantine's office, a speckled gray tortoise-shell cat greeted them at the door. They took off their fleece coats and sat down. The cat jumped up on the corner of the desk.

Barrantine could feel the tension.

"I hope you don't mind that I brought my cat to the office. Mazzy is her name."

"We love cats," said Ana.

"How were the roads?" asked Barrantine.

"Not good, not good at all. We got in an argument on the way over."

Martin turned to Ana and apologized for his cutting words, apologized for the storm, for the ice, for the discord in himself. Meanwhile, Mazzy hopped off the desk, walked over to the pedestal near the black box and began rubbing on it.

"How have things been going otherwise?" asked Barrantine.

Ana reached over and grabbed Martin's hand. "There's been a major life stressor this week. Martin's father is in the hospital."

"I'm sorry," said Barrantine. "What happened?"

"His liver is shutting down," said Martin. "He's been an alcoholic for a long time."

"Does he live here in Denver?"

"Yep, but I don't see him much, and we're not real close. I was raised by my mom in Seattle."

"I see. And did you spend any time with your father growing up?"

"He used to visit me on occasion, and I used to come down to Denver for a couple weeks during the summers."

"And when you got older, did you move here to be closer to your father?" asked Barrantine.

"No, it was just coincidence that I ended up here in Denver. My dad had nothing to do with it."

"And your mother? Does she still live in Seattle?"

"Yep, still there."

"Can you tell me a little bit about her?"

"Well, she's Polish, actually, and came over to America in her early 20s. She started a cleaning business, which is how she met my dad. She used to clean his office. My dad ran a small construction business in Seattle."

"And is your dad Polish as well?"

"No, he's black."

"Were your parents together for long?"

"A few years, I believe. It was kind of on-again, off-again. They never married."

"Sorry for all the questions, yet I think it's worth spending some time talking about your background. I take it that your father moved to Denver after they broke up?"

"Basically. He went to work at his brother's restaurant, to be part owner and whatnot. He probably wanted to get away from my mom as well. She's a little crazy." Martin laughed.

"Crazy?"

"Yeah, as in emotionally unstable. I think my mom has a mood disorder like borderline personality."

"What made you come to this conclusion?"

"I don't know. She's just very self-absorbed. Growing up, everything ran through her emotional needs. Even when she's wrong, she's right. That kind of thing. She's good at turning stuff around, making it seem like it's everyone else's fault. Guilt tripping, I guess. My mom is good at guilt tripping."

Barrantine paged though his journal and drew a picture of a person standing in a field with two ravens flying overhead. "And your parents, Ana? How is your relationship with your mother and father?"

"Oh, there's not really much to say. I had a good upbringing. It wasn't perfect by any stretch, but my parents were supportive."

"Do they live here in Denver as well?"

"My mom lives in New Mexico. My father passed away years ago." Ana fiddled with her purse.

"That must have been difficult," said Barrantine. "And what did your parents do for a living?"

"My father was a university math professor, my mother a stay-at-home mom. No brothers or sisters."

"Are you close to your mother? Do you see her often?"

"She comes to visit once a year, and we visit her. My relationship with my mother is good, much different than Martin's."

"True," said Martin, staring out the window. "Haven't seen my mom for two years."

"And your dad? Have you visited him in the hospital?"

"Nah, not yet, and not sure if I will. What's really left to say? My dad has basically ruined his life."

"Do you have a theory about why? Was he always an alcoholic?"

"No, not always. He was more moderate earlier in his life. Even used to lift weights, play different sports, etc. I think the heavy drinking started after he had a falling-out with his brother, right around when the restaurant shut down. From there, he got into trouble with the law. Might have even been homeless for a while, or that's what my mom told me. I guess that's when his demons started to come out."

20 – Pastor Samuel on the Storm

After the violent storm, Angel Neurons began emerging from their rooms. Pastor Samuel tiptoed into the kitchen. Nate was hunched over the Plexiglas watching for changes in the weather. Pastor Samuel could see that his son had not slept and had dark circles under his eyes. Yet at the center of Nate's pupils, he noticed a faint sparkle, an exuberance of spirit.

"Good morning, Son. How are you?"

"I'm good, Dad. I was up late last night."

"What were you doing?"

"Watching the Storm. The lightning strikes were awe-inspiring."

Pastor Samuel sat in a chair next to Nate and looked down through the Plexiglas floor, where pink clouds reflected a sheen over the surface of the Sea. Although the vastness of the open water made it difficult to identify anything specific, at times Angel Neurons noticed small flecks of colored light or dark oblong shapes. Not today. The water was calm, distant, like a faraway galaxy a billion light years away.

"Son, I know the Storm and the Sea can appear beautiful, but let's not forget how violent they truly are. Like many things referenced in scripture, these are not places for creatures like ourselves to ponder too much."

"I understand. Or at least I understand the mythology of it. But it is an amazing sight, the Storm, the Sea, the Sky. Wouldn't it be interesting to learn why the Storm exists, why it clears on certain days and not on others? Wouldn't it be cool to know what is in the Sea?"

Pastor Samuel squinted. Normally he would reprimand Nate for his scriptures-as-myth comment, but he knew his son was too far along on his journey to correct this.

"The Book tells us about unfathomable darkness down there," said Pastor Samuel. "I'm not sure I want to know any more."

"That's true, Dad, but the Book also says flying insects have four legs."

"Nathaniel, there is no place for so much sarcasm."

"I'm sorry, Dad."

"I forgive you, Son." Pastor Samuel placed his hand on Nate's shoulder. "I believe the Storm clears in relation to sin."

"What do you mean?"

"Well, the Book tells us that Hell is related to sin. I have often speculated that the Storm has something to do with Hell. Maybe when the Storm clears, there are lessons being learned in the greater universe. When it becomes more intense, a sort of evil is taking place. So, perhaps the Storm has a symbolic quality representing the state of the universe, the state of sin and redemption."

"And how do you think the Sea factors in?"

"My thought is that the Sea is where dark creatures exist, creatures that push us to the heart of sin itself. Demons, monsters, beasts of all sorts. It is the most dangerous place of all, even more dangerous than the Storm because it is inhabited by dark creatures; it has life. Maybe the Sea is Hell itself."

"Dad, is this specifically written in the Book?"

"No, Son. It's just a theory I have based on my own interpretation."

Nate appreciated the creativity of his father's explanation.

"That's interesting, Dad, but how would we know what the outside world is really like when we are trapped in the Plexiglas?"

"Trapped? I wouldn't use that word. Without this structure, we'd certainly fall to our deaths. It is the very thing keeping us alive, keeping us safe. Son, the Plexiglas is not just our home; it is a form of self-defense."

56

21 – One-Sentence Time Machine

Although the weather had warmed considerably, the mountains had a shadowy, foreboding quality, as if a storm was on the way. Swiveling back-and-forth in his chair, Barrantine placed his hands on the black box that rested on his desk. In the background, a dark silhouette of the Front Range loomed in the window.

"Good afternoon, glad to see you. What a sunset, huh?" Barrantine gestured toward the window, but his eyes never left Martin and Ana. "I wanted to remind you that this will be our last group session for a while. Our next appointment will be an individual session. We can schedule that later."

Barrantine tapped his fingers on the black box. "You are probably wondering what this device is sitting in front of me."

"An amplifier?" asked Martin.

"No, no, this is not music-related. This is quite different. It's actually an invention. Well, it's not patented yet, but that's only because I've chosen to keep the technology under wraps." Barrantine lifted the lid on the black box and extracted three watches from inside the machine. "What you have in front of you is the control center for a set of watches that allow us to monitor our communication."

"Monitor our communication?" asked Martin slowly.

Barrantine placed one of the watches around his wrist. "Yes, with these small timepieces, it is possible for a person to retract words, and indeed entire sentences, from the fabric of reality, so as to avoid any potentially harmful consequences. With the push of a button, the watches can turn back the clock on our words. In short, these are time travel devices based on language and intentionality. So, say you have an argument and utter a hurtful sentence. You push the button, and that hurtful sentence is gone. Given your recent arguments, I thought this could be useful. I've seen the watches work wonders in relationships."

Martin's mouth flopped open.

"Yes, I understand this must be shocking," continued Barrantine. "Who would have imagined such an invention was possible, right? But I am here to say that the technology works. It hasn't come easy, but it works. The machine is based on my doctoral studies in the metaphysics of language. I also borrowed heavily from Ludwig Wittgenstein's development of truth tables. To be more precise, the watches tap into the underlying quantum makeup of our brains, which allows for the time reversal. What I've discovered is that when we roll back the clock on our words, a new outcome will often emerge, which is to say, new words will leave our mouths, and an entirely new future can take shape. Again, this is due to the unpredictable nature of quantum indeterminacy."

Barrantine handed a watch to Martin and Ana. "Are you interested in trying the One-Sentence Time Machine technology? Shall we give it a go?"

They placed the watches on their wrists.

"Very good. Here's how this works. When you push the black button on the face of the watch, time moves backwards exactly in relation to a single sentence that one person has uttered and another person has heard."

"Huh?" said Martin.

"Yes, so suppose you say something you regret, for example, a comment that might be unnecessarily cutting. After said comment is uttered, you can push the button and extinguish the sentence from the reality of those involved."

"This works only with single sentences?" asked Martin.

"Right, the metaphysics, the logical and empirical conditions, allow for one sentence at most." Barrantine pulled on his ear neurotically.

"And does it work for exactly two people?" asked Ana.

"Good question. It can work for more than two people, but it depends on who the sentence was directed to. So, the intentionality itself is part of the time reversal."

"Does the sentence have to be grammatical?" asked Martin.

"Sort of. The sentence must have some semblance of proper grammar, and slang words are acceptable. Thank goodness, right, as these are the words we often want to erase." Barrantine chuckled to himself. "Shall we give it a test run?"

Martin and Ana nodded.

"Ana, let me first illustrate this with you. Now, please forgive the extreme nature of what I'm about to say, and please forgive the sideways humor. But I think you will understand that in order for me to convince you of the efficacy of the One-Sentence Time Machine, I will need to say something outlandish. Perhaps a bit of slightly deviant humor in counseling is also helpful."

Dr. Barrantine adjusted his seat.

"Are you ready?"

"Yes."

"Ana, please listen carefully. Note that neither Martin nor I will have any memory of this sentence after I push the button. Or, well, I may remember parts, but this is only because of my second-order experiences with the technology. Okay, here we go. Martin, the dinner you cooked for Ana the other night tasted like rotten sewer sludge."

Martin's face contorted.

Ana's eyes grew bright.

Dr. Barrantine pushed the button.

The sentence "~~Martin, the dinner you cooked for Ana the other tonight tasted like rotten sewer sludge~~" was extinguished from reality.

Martin's expression reverted back to its prior state, as did Barrantine's. Ana wore a sly smile on her face, as if this alone had a healing effect on their marriage.

"Now, in order to illustrate this to Martin, I would also like to try this with you, Ana. Remember that after I utter the sentence and push the button, time will move backwards for you and me. However, Martin will still remember the sentence, and thus time will not move backwards for him."

Ana's smile turned to a frown.

"Are you ready, Ana?"

"Sure. This sentence isn't going to be like the last one, is it?" she asked.

"No, no, not at all. It won't have anything to do with cooking. All right, ready, here we go."

Barrantine moved forward in his chair and scanned Ana's appearance. "The checked shirt you are wearing resembles an old quilt my gramma made back in the '50s."

Ana had a disgusted, deeply offended look on her face, as if her personal space had been violated and she wanted a refund on the counseling.

Martin's mood instantly lightened.

Barrantine pushed the button.

The sentence "~~The checkered skirt you are wearing resembles an old quilt my gramma made back in the '50s~~" was wiped clean from the fabric of existence as it pertained to Ana's conscious experience.

"Do both of you understand how it works?" asked Barrantine.

"Yes," they said.

"And are you interested in giving it a try in your personal lives? I'd say it stands a good chance of being a welcome addition to your relationship. Sometimes all it takes is the retraction of a single sentence, and the entire course of an evening can change."

Martin and Ana agreed to give it a try.

"Very good then. Now, I would urge you to use this sparingly. When you have said or texted something you regret—and to clarify, the machine does work on phones—simply push the button, and a different outcome may occur. Again, this is due to quantum indeterminacy. Even though the initial conditions are identical, the very structure of the subatomic particles in our brains—electrons, quarks, etc.—will act in fundamentally unpredictable ways. Although physicists and philosophers have long argued that quantum indeterminacy cannot be seen in our actual experience, we finally have empirical proof at the macro level of consciousness."

22 – Martin Tries the Watch

Martin secured the One-Sentence Time Machine watch to his wrist, placed the vaporizer pen to his lips and inhaled the Moby Dick indica strain. Feeling pleasantly high and nostalgic, he hit play on Nirvana's *Nevermind* and started slicing tomatillos to the crashing sounds of "Smells Like Teen Spirit."

His cell phone rang. Ana was on her way home from work. She wanted to know if he would bring the trash out to the street because tomorrow was garbage day. Martin paused and adjusted the One-Sentence Time Machine. This was the first time he would use it, and there was a certain freedom he felt from having it on. For a person who often said things he regretted, it was nice to have a safety net for his words. Martin wondered if Barrantine had invented something truly revolutionary.

"What was that? What did you say?" asked Martin.

"I was wondering if you could take the trash out to the street? Tomorrow is trash day."

Martin cleared his throat. Time to take the time travel device for a spin.

"The trash can take itself out to the damn street."

"What?!" Ana stepped hard on the pedal of her Toyota Prius.

Martin pushed the button on the One-Sentence Time Machine watch.

The sentence "~~The trash can take itself out to the damn street~~" was forever wiped clean from the face of existence, as was Ana's pressing down on the gas pedal.

"Sure, I'll go ahead and take the trash out right now," said Martin, the randomness of the subatomic particles in his brain giving him a different result. Everything was kosher. The One-Sentence Time Machine worked like a charm.

Martin browned a pork loin then added green chilies, tomatillos, chicken stock, garlic, onions, jalapenos and spices to the pot. The gorgeous green concoction boiled away, as Kurt Cobain sang in the background.

Ana walked through the door. Pleased to see that the trash had been taken out to the street, she placed her purse on the counter. However, Martin had forgot their recycling. An empty wine bottle, a milk carton and two soup cans were on the counter from the previous night.

"Hi babe, smells great in here. What are you making?" she asked.

"Green chili burritos."

"Yum." Ana turned her attention to the recycling. "Let me take that out," she said, in a passive-aggressive tone.

Martin looked up from the pot of green chili simmering on the stove. "Don't you think you should, you know, use your device?" he said.

"What?" asked Ana, letting out a breath of air in frustration.

Martin pushed the button.

The sentence "~~Don't you think you should, you know, use your device?~~" was tallywacked from the essence of the room. Mission accomplished. Again, the unpredictable nature of the subatomic particles in Martin's brain led to a different conscious cognition.

"You know what, babe," said Martin. "Let me go ahead and take the recycling out. I forgot."

They sat down for dinner. Martin felt optimistic about the watches. During the next session, he even considered pushing for an upgraded time travel device, one that was capable of deleting several sentences at once. Imagine the problems we could solve in relationships if multiple sentences, even entire paragraphs, could be scrubbed clean from our lives.

After dinner, Ana did her normal routine of taking an evening shower, while Martin watched one of his favorite shows, the *Deadliest Catch*. Immersed in the episode, he took a blast from his vaporizer and pictured himself standing on the deck of the *Northwestern*, facing danger and isolation in the pounding seas, exposed yet fully engaged, senses on high alert, waiting for the elusive crustacean to rise from the depths of the Bering Sea.

Something about the *Deadliest Catch* sparked Martin's imagination, made him feel more connected to the world and to the Sisyphean questions it posed about meaning and suffering in the absence of a grand narrative. It was perplexing that crabbers chose such an unforgiving lifestyle, Martin thought. Odd that they suffered the same way year in and year out. Eighteen-hour shifts. Hands swollen. Blood and salt leaching from their pours.

Did crabbers possess a hidden category of perception?

Was their rendezvous with the Bering Sea a shout-out to the paradoxical nature of pain itself?

The show ended.

Now flipping through cooking channels, Martin's mind moved to an entirely different question. How could he elicit feelings of sexual pleasure in Ana? Martin often grew amorous this time of night. But would Ana be open to his advances? Would she be in the mood?

Ana strolled through the living room in a towel, her curves making Martin's pulse elevate.

"Babe, your body looks nice," said Martin.

"I'm feeling really overweight," responded Ana.

"You look great. I like it when you walk through the house with a towel. And I like it when you are overweight." Wait a minute, what? Martin pushed the button.

"~~And I like it when you are overweight~~" vanished from the room.

"Your curves are amazing," he said.

Ana returned to the bathroom and began blow-drying her hair.

Sensing a novel opportunity, Martin stood up from the couch and walked over.

"I want you," he said, clutching her from behind. "I want you badly." Dirty thoughts rushed in.

She turned and kissed him. The kiss was nice but had little passion. Martin's hands moved down Ana's stomach as she stood in front of the mirror. He led her into the bedroom, began kissing her neck, her breasts, the inside of her thighs, in search of erotic sex, stormy sex, sex with lightning and hail, animal to animal, the erasing of all rational thought.

But Ana wasn't having it, and the sex ended up being straightforward and missionary. Pure eroticism wasn't on the menu. Lovemaking was. As well as identification and interpersonal growth, the desire to feel the original bond that brought them together, to connect entirely, synchronize fully. To find that place where carnality and commitment can hold hands, swim in the same part of the Sea.

23 – Banshee and the Sperm Whale

Near a craggy hogback at the base of Martin's limbic system, where his dentate gyrus collided with his hippocampus like two tectonic plates, a lumbering animal moved through the aquamarine blue. As it passed in front of Banshee, the great leviathan made a wall of blackness that blocked the Diver Neuron's line of sight for what seemed like minutes.

Desmond placed a dendrite on Chuck. "What is it?" he said, his voice quivering.

"I believe it's a sperm whale," said Chuck, noticing distinctive scars along the whale's flukes. "And I don't like this one bit."

Chuck looked back at the rest of the Diver Neurons, who continued to push forward, their minds flooded with sexual thoughts about Banshee—her puffy lips, the tiptoeing motion of her tail when she swam, curves that went on for days. Sure, there was danger in tangling with a mysterious mermaid, and yes, hypersexual creatures like themselves did have a lower life expectancy, but the possibility of watching a woman go elbows to knees made a neuron's mind go blank.

Zeke stepped to the front of the line. Bruised and battered, with cuts and abrasions across his cell body from the battles he'd waged at the back of the line, the inner-city kid stepped up to Chuck and got in his face, as if he wanted to challenge Chuck's authority full-stop.

"What we gonna do with this damn whale?" he asked, blond dreads shooting from his head like the tentacles on a sea anemone.

"We are going to let it be," said Chuck. "It's not a threat to us."

"This dude trying to get up in our shit, man."

"No, it isn't," said Chuck. "It's way too big for her."

Zeke took the reference the wrong way. *Big.* The sperm whale got a big dick. Bigger than his. Chuck is gonna let this sperm whale come up in here and cock-block us with its big dick and ugly-ass block for a head.

Ironically, the Diver Neurons were clueless about the true nature of sperm whales, including what the "sperm" in their name referred to. They had always supposed "sperm" referred to a white substance produced from the whale's sex organs, when in fact the waxy substance inside the whale's skull was most likely used for buoyancy or echolocation. Not only this, but sperm whales were peaceful, harmonious creatures who liked to observe and showed little interest in mermaids.

Banshee swam closer. "Are you really gonna let this sperm whale have me?"

At this point, Chuck sensed true danger. Even though sexual thoughts walloped his consciousness just like the next guy, Banshee struck him as almost *too* perfect, her densely lubricated center just a little too intoxicating. Sure, she might be just the slut they'd hoped, but Banshee seemed to want it too badly.

A huge wave pounded the surface of the Sea.

Another one.

The sky above grew dark. A reverse undertow began to push the Diver Neurons upward toward Banshee's womanhood. All it would take is one wrong move, one miscalculated slip of the willy, and billions of Diver Neurons could perish. Billions. Maybe the entire expedition. Just like that. Because that's how bad things happen. They happen when they do. Such is their nature. To catch you off guard, exploit you when you are vulnerable, send you into oblivion when you least expect it.

24 – Martin's Childhood

After a long day of prepping vegetables for the salad bar, Martin drove to his solo counseling session with Dr. Barrantine. His eyes heavy from sleep deprivation, Martin wondered why he had scheduled this appointment when Ana was in San Diego. He could have used more free time to totally let down, blow off steam. Not another obligation, another box to check. But even if he were free, what would constitute a satisfying letdown? Exercise? A healthy meal? A movie? No. Those all sounded like chores.

Martin pulled into the Falling Rock taproom, ordered a pint of Rogue's White Whale Ale. For some reason, Seattle was on his mind, more specifically his mother. The distance that had grown between them over the years. The distance that had started to expand on the day he was born. He hadn't talked to her for months. Was she still married to the same loser who operated the forklift on the docks? Did she realize Ana's birthday was last week?

Martin finished his beer. He ordered another. *There, much better*, he said to himself, the beer tumbling down his throat like glacier water. *Ready to talk about life*. Although sarcasm tinted Martin's self-talk, the fatigue began to lift. He got in his car and drove to Barrantine's.

"So, tell me," said Barrantine, "have you been using the One-Sentence Time Machine?"

Martin pulled up his sleeve. "Wearing it now."

"Has it been working?"

"Yeah, it's been helpful. Just not sure how long I will be able to rely on it."

"Understood. The device is useful, but has its limitations.

While it can help increase awareness of our words so we can better predict and modify our behaviors, eventually one must take the watch off."

Barrantine noticed an impatience of spirit in Martin and documented it in his journal.

"In general, how have things been going for you over the last week or two? How is your father doing? Is he still in the hospital?"

"No, he's out of the hospital and doing better. My dad's got an iron constitution."

"Did you end up ever visiting him?"

"No, I just called."

Martin's phone buzzed in his pocket. He resisted checking it, but Barrantine heard the buzz and could smell alcohol in the air. He slid open the curtains, cracked the window. Dark clouds formed outside. Thunder in the distance.

"Looks like the spring storms are coming early."

"Early?" said Martin. "I guess so."

"I'm glad to hear your dad is doing better. Did you have a good conversation with him?"

"Not really. I just told him that I was thinking about him and wished him well."

"Martin, do you mind if we talk more about your father?"

"That's fine."

"So, when you were younger, I'm talking middle school, early teens here, how would you characterize your relationship with your father? Was it distant? Warm? Did you have strong feelings for him?"

Martin rubbed his temples. "I guess it was fine. Nothing major to report. I did look up to him at that age, and I actually wanted to move to Denver, but it never happened."

"Why?"

"Because my mom wouldn't let me leave. She was insecure, wanted to control me. Probably wanted the child support."

"And did your dad want you to move out?"

"He said he did."

"Is this when your relationship with your father took a downward turn?"

"I'd say so. Basically, he stopped visiting, or visited very little, anyway. I never visited either, not that I can recall."

"I see. Now, fast-forward to when you moved to Denver. I take it that you got reacquainted with your father?"

"I wouldn't say reacquainted. He was a drunk by the time I moved here, not the person I knew as a kid. His hands shook badly." Martin fiddled with one of his own hands. "They still do. When you see these struggles in a parent, you don't want to go down the same road. Thankfully, my dad and I come from very different backgrounds."

Barrantine laced his fingers together. "In what respect?"

"Like, I wasn't raised in the hood...he was."

"What kind of neighborhood were you raised in?"

"Middle-class, basically."

"Did this cause any discord with your father?"

Martin considered the question carefully. "I wouldn't say discord. I think he wanted me to have a good life. But he did like to joke that I wasn't all black."

"And how did this make you feel?"

"I laughed."

"And would you say that you identify more with your mother and her Polish heritage?"

"No. I grew up eating pierogis, but they were frozen, and I boiled them. My mom never even turned on the stove." Martin snickered.

"Your mother has her own cleaning business, correct?"

"Yep, house cleaning."

Martin's phone buzzed in his pocket.

"Is she remarried?"

"She's been married three times."

"So you were raised with different father figures in your life?"

"There were a few stepfathers and boyfriends."

"Tell me about these stepfathers and boyfriends."

"Not much to say. A few were pretty cool, others not so much."

"And with these men who were not so cool, what tended to be the problem?"

"I just think as a young boy, I felt like I was competing with them—competing for my mom's attention. I guess at that time in my life, I felt like I really needed her."

"When did your feelings change?"

"Oh, at a young age, probably ten or eleven years old. Right around the time I started to realize my mom didn't really want a kid. Right around when she started getting intense with me."

"Intense? Do you mean abusive?"

"Yeah, and kinda nutty."

"Can you give me an example?"

"One of her boyfriends once cut the crotches out of her underwear and left them on the kitchen table with a note written in lipstick that said Polack Witch."

"I see," said Barrantine, placing a hand over his mouth. "And what effect do you think this had on you?"

"Not sure. I suppose I don't like witches. Ha, ha. Seriously, though, I have a hard time being around large groups of people, all the energy, you know. Not sure if it applies."

Barrantine pursed his lips together. "In light of your childhood, I can understand why you might have a hard time filtering information. Because you were exposed to this abusive intensity and empty parenting, this could make it difficult for you to put that bubble around yourself that everyone needs as an adult." Barrantine grabbed a tissue from his desk drawer and wiped his forehead. "And what were your high school years like? What happened after high school?"

"Starting around my freshman year, I went down bad paths—drinking, stealing, just doing stupid shit. Like I said, my mom wasn't keeping tabs on me, so I was running wild, hanging with friends, skateboarding through downtown Seattle at all hours of the night. I ended up dropping out of high school my junior year and getting a GED."

"Then what?"

"Then I got a job at a fine-dining Italian restaurant, which changed my life."

"Cooking?"

"Yeah, cooking."

"I recall from a prior conversation that you mentioned the possibility of borderline personality disorder in your mother. Any other history of psychological illness in your family?"

"Not that I'm aware of. I mean, both of my parents probably suffer from something. Both were raised in tough families. I can't remember if I mentioned it, but my grandfather on my mom's side had post-traumatic stress disorder after World War II."

Dr. Barrantine jotted down notes in his journal. Although Martin seemed to be a thoughtful guy with a good head on his shoulders, Barrantine suspected that he suffered from a type of post-traumatic stress disorder similar to his grandfather. Further, he theorized that the disorder was presenting itself unconsciously in the byzantine structures of Martin's grey matter, where cultural or racial complexities helped shape his brain in novel ways. Barrantine reached in his drawer, grabbed a midnight-blue colored pencil and began sketching a giant sea squid on the back of his journal.

25 – Pressure Mounts for Chuck

The Diver Neurons had never seen the Sea exhibit such strange hues. Mustard brown riffles. Peppered granules of organic matter. Cherry-red bubbles that carried Banshee's intoxicating scent. Mesmerized by her feminine parts, Chuck adjusted his dive belt, tried to gain focus and seek a sensible course of action. Thankfully, the sperm whale was swimming away, and Zeke had fallen back, so at least Chuck had some time to reflect.

Desmond patted Chuck on the shoulder. "What should we do, boss?"

Chuck surveyed the broken line of Diver Neurons, where distant screams could be heard and blood trails traced upward like mealy worms. "All right, no one's going to like this, but we're moving on. We're gonna abort the mission."

"Are you sure?" Desmond gestured to the raging pattern of testosterone that zig-zagged in the water. "I thought we were going to see this through."

"I've changed my mind. I don't trust this mermaid one bit, and the whole sperm whale situation gave me a bad vibe. When's the last time we've seen one of those?"

"Do you want me to go tell the others?" asked Desmond.

"I guess that's probably not a bad idea. I'll stay here and watch Banshee. Are you okay with breaking the news to everyone?"

"I'm fine with it, boss. I think it's going to get worse if we don't act soon." Desmond paused. "Ummm...the other thing I wanted to say is I'm sorry for not doing a better job with Zeke. Being from the same neighborhood and all, I thought your plan made sense, but Zeke never bought in. Know what I mean?"

Chuck reached over and patted Desmond on the shoulder. "It's not your fault, Dez. You can lead a seahorse to its food source but you can't make it eat. Make no mistake, though, you were a great mentor, and he was lucky to have you. But when the water settles, I believe we might have to take a new approach. I'm not sure if Zeke is going to be with us anymore. Just be careful."

"Ten-four."

Desmond turned and swam in the direction of Zeke and his crew. When he arrived on the scene, Zeke was waving his dendrites around manically in conversation with a huge pack of Diver Neurons.

"So, I was talking to Chuck," said Desmond, "and he decided we can't trust this mermaid. For safety reasons, he thinks we better leave."

"Leave?" asked Zeke, getting up in Desmond's grill. "We got a perfectly good piece of ass in front of us, and Chuck thinks we outta leave?"

"Yes," affirmed Desmond. "He reckons it's the smart move. It's not worth risking it for a single mermaid. There are other fish in the sea."

Zeke's eyes were bloodshot and distant. "And who do you think you are, man? The messenger...second in command? Nah, I'll tell you who you are. You Chuck's little bitch."

Desmond shook his head back-and-forth. "Whatever, man."

Meanwhile, Banshee, who had been watching closely, swam over. Aroused by the chaos, she began touching herself, moaning, screaming out in pre-orgasmic pleasure, which sent Zeke into a kind of carnal sexual autopilot, his mind charcoal black.

Zeke cocked his arm back as far as he could and with the

force of a steel kettleball struck Desmond on the side of his head. With one huge blow, Dez was knocked out cold, his limp body floating up where the Sea convulsed and the waves broke heavy.

26 – Barrantine on Martin

Dr. Barrantine poured himself a glass of wine from the Infinite Monkey Theorem. He paged through his journal and began highlighting key words. Seeking clarity in his diagnosis of Martin, he hoped that the uncontrolled motion of the pen could advance his thinking to new places.

Deviant texting

Hypersexuality

Problem drinking

Pornography

Destructive ways of dealing with boredom

Poor impulse control

Underactive regulative control centers of the brain

The internal world of the psyche

The inaccessible parts of the self

Only the body truly knows

Quantum chaos

Barrantine swirled the wine around in his glass and repeated each word silently in his head. Other words followed.

Metaphor

The spell childhood casts over our lives

The spell living in our bodies

Living in our brains

The inner-outer world gap

The mind-body problem

For a minute, Barrantine reflected on his early days as an

undergrad when he had devoured books on the ontology of mind. In the end, he was a committed materialist, a steadfast supporter of neuroscience—the mind *was* the brain. But he had a translation problem. The mind and the brain do not speak the same language. Consciousness does not fully reduce to mere physical descriptions. Yet it was the unconscious that troubled Barrantine most. While unconscious brain activity could be detected on an fMRI scan, this did not help in a clinical setting, where it was necessary to discuss that which is suppressed, that which is inaccessible.

How do we access and penetrate the hidden fabric of our grey matter?

The destructive impulses
The unconscious facticity of our youth
Of race
Of identity
Of pain
Of disconnectedness from family
Of unrealized love

Barrantine took a long pull on the Cab Franc blend and affirmed his diagnosis. Martin did indeed suffer from a kind of post-traumatic stress disorder that issued from the deviant logic of his childhood, where he was duped, or at least strongly influenced, by unconscious forces. And so, the challenge for the counselor was to tap into these unconscious forces indirectly through discussion, questions, narrative representations, behavioral modifications, symbols, metaphors, therapeutic inventions—all while factoring in the wild-card effects of quantum indeterminacy.

Yet, even though Barrantine now felt clearer in his general

approach, he also sensed a danger lurking within Martin. He sensed this danger because he knew it in himself. He knew the perils of counseling, the pitfalls of self-analysis. He knew the duplicitous nature of unconscious forces, their cunning, their ability to respond to adversity, their impact, their patterns, their adaptive nature, the way in which they can provoke regrettable actions under the guise of normalcy. The question was how to head the destruction forces off at the pass before it was too late.

Part 3: Falling Through the Storm

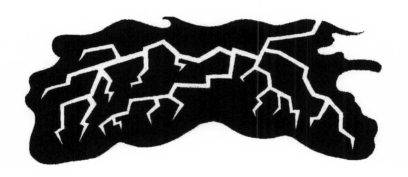

27 – Denver Flood

Martin drove away from his counseling session with Barrantine. Heading south on Colorado Boulevard, he passed by an old rundown brick house that reminded him of his home in Seattle, where he pictured his mother sitting on the couch with a cigarette and a gin and tonic, half tanked, half asleep, half full of briny emotion. Martin didn't even tell Barrantine about the uglier stuff with his mother. Like when she left Martin home alone for two straight days at age twelve. Or when she forgot to lock the bedroom door, and Martin stumbled upon the next-door neighbor, a married man, taking her from behind. Or the yelling. Or the cocaine. Or the fuck you, dick, asshole, deadbeat comments aimed at Martin's father.

It was sad Martin couldn't pick up the phone and call her, process all the pain and animosity, in the hope of moving forward. Or maybe he could swing by his father's place, have a drink with him, or better yet a conversation, a real one. Even if they just batted around the ugly stuff, what could have been, something would be better than nothing. Maybe it would help them feel less alone in the world, less riddled by feelings of inadequacy and contradictory thoughts. Who knows, they might even have a laugh.

Martin picked up his phone and shot off a text to Ana.

"I hope you enjoyed your last day at the conference," he said. "Just finished up with counselling."

"Thank you, the conference was...very conference like," she said, followed by a bug-eyed emoji.

"I hear you. Off to grab dinner," Martin typed back.

"Okay, enjoy your alone time. Be good! I love you."

"I love you too. See you tomorrow."

Martin turned left on Colfax, just to do a little sightseeing, just to have a look-see down the longest road in America. Passing by several dive bars and strip clubs, his head rubbernecked to watch every woman, every hooker he could. One of the women waved him forward. He slowed down, turned off on a side street. As she approached, Martin pulled away, just for fun.

A couple miles further east on Colfax, he pulled into the Hangar Bar parking lot. Stepping inside, he sat down at the bar and ordered a drink, a double gin and tonic to match his mood, to toast his own freedom. His fingers loose, Martin started texting. No one watched. No one cared. No obligations. He could just be. Move through time, release his pent-up energy, under the influence, the contents of his consciousness stewarded away like a ship at sea.

"Hey," his fingers typed.

"Where's your ball and chain at?" replied Marguerite.

"San Diego," he responded, the words on his iPhone gathering, churning, feeling like they could go anywhere the Storm took them. Martin's temporal lobe became dim, covered by haze, by the dark glow of the sky.

"Whatchu want? Wanna hang out? Wanna grab a drink?"

Martin put his phone in his pocket but it buzzed several more times, buzzed along his frontal lobe, where the creative parts of himself, the little outbursts of the artist, flew through turbulent skies. *Did his mother and father know they had encouraged this inner darkness in their son?*

"It's starting to rain pretty hard," said the tender to Martin. "Wasn't supposed to rain today."

The sky grew black. The rain pelted down hard, strangely hard, out the bottom of a topless cloudbank. His space for thinking now more limited, Martin's perspective was hemmed in by the passionate movement of the Storm.

Martin placed a ten on the bar and left. Texting as he drove, he fiddled with the One-Sentence Time Machine on his wrist, pushing it frequently after lewd comments. It was a game. It was fun. His alcohol-induced framework encouraged it. The world presented itself lightly, like the present moment was all that mattered.

"Does it turn you on that I have a wife?" he sent.

Martin pushed the button on the One-Sentence Time Machine.

The sentence "~~Does it turn you on that I have a wife?~~" vanished into thin air.

"Do you want her to watch?"

Martin pushed the button.

"~~Do you want her to watch?~~" left like a bad habit.

"Are you wet?"

This time Martin did not push the button on the One-Sentence Time Machine.

"Very," said Marguerite.

Martin's heart beat fast; his entire body pulsed. His lower regions went boom, boom, boom when they should have been still. Freedom was the dominant thought, and nothing else mattered, including the consequences of his own freedom, which were covered by the Storm, now in two places. Inside and out, above and within, about to spill over, drown him out completely.

The rain crashed down hard onto the windshield as he drove; the wipers sliced back-and-forth like dueling swords. Puddles formed on the street. Martin drove under an old railroad line. The water rose half past his tires. For a second, the heavy rain told him to stop, that going home was the only sensible decision, that anything else would be deceitful, not right, the product of shadows.

Martin continued to text, and the giving away of words became easier. Easier because he could take them back. And Martin now missed far too many sentences and just let the lewd words escape his head and enter the world like an oil spill. He didn't really mean what he said, but when words leave us, they take on a certain reality. They become us in new ways. Change our course of action. Change the very makeup of our brains and our identity. Change the future. Barrantine was right.

Martin stopped using the One-Sentence Time Machine and pulled over to the exact place that his words took him. A park. He reclined the seat back. The rain continued to fall hard, soaking his words, making them stay down, become unconscious.

Martin opened the door of his Nissan Rogue for Marguerite, who lowered her umbrella and sat down. He leaned back in his seat even more, leaned back as far as he could go, and stared out the window at the basketball court in front of him. The basketball court that looked like a lake. A lake that was alive in the way a dream was alive. Did a fish jump? Did a shadow move over its surface?

The only thing distinct was a silver pole for the basketball hoop. Water crystals illuminated by street lights ran down the pole. Down. Down. Down. The silver pole was hard. Hard as steel ever got. For a minute, Martin reflected on how hard a steel pole could get. Hard enough to dunk a basketball on, that's for sure. But how would he know? Martin sucked at basketball and couldn't dunk to save his life.

Rain continued to rip through the sky and move down the pole. Down, down, down, in a steady cadence. Up, up, up. Faster. Thunder boomed through the interior of the car, loud like a steel drum. Rain turned into hail. Ten thousand pelts per minute. Police sirens sounded off. Car alarms.

Honk. Honk. Honk.

The basketball court continued to fill up. The lake grew big. Up, up, up it went. Down, down, down came the rain, along with hail. Up, down, up, down, up, down. Martin breathed deeply. The entire park was ready to explode. A lightning bolt struck down in front of them. Another followed. Another. Marguerite stayed focused.

On the brink of a massive weather system, the park began sinking under water. Martin closed his eyes, tried to relax and weather the storm. But he had a headache, and the headache pounded in the back of his head, where serotonin levels were dangerously low, and where his moral compass was cracked, full of water, overworked, beaten down by something vicious. Something hidden. A Temptress who had snuck in the back door of his consciousness, started disrespecting him, making him feel like less of a person, less of a man, provoking the Satyr in him to respond to her exploits. To the mental games she was playing. To the bright color of pain that was bleeding out from within.

28 – Zeke Goes Off

His groin burning like a three-alarm fire, Zeke stood nose to nose with Chuck. Despite the utter seriousness of the situation and being worried about Desmond, Chuck could not wholly disregard the power of Banshee. Though his best friend had just been beaten down by a thug with no self-understanding, Chuck wanted to fuck this bow-legged ho as much as the next guy. And at that moment, he was no better than Zeke, no better at all. His cock no less hard, Chuck was Zeke, Zeke was Chuck in a certain respect.

"Come on," said Banshee in Echolocation. "*Cum on*," she enunciated, her legs spread wide, her juicy, wet, orange sea sponge inviting them in.

The neuronal hairs of the Diver Neurons grew erect.

The pheromone molecules in the water blazed with the power of a thousand suns.

Chuck sensed the darkest capabilities of his own kind. Only the hunt mattered. The glorious orange sea sponge. The jet-black hair, stiletto heels, lipstick, tits that went on for days. The hottest mermaid on record, time to dip their wicks in her fat ass.

"Let's do this!" yelled Zeke.

"No," said Chuck, shaking his head. "No," he said louder. "Fall back."

The huge wall of twenty billion neurons gathered behind Zeke while he fixated on Chuck. Many wanted to give Chuck the opportunity to speak up, so he could change his course of action, be a productive member of the team. He'd done a lot for them after all. Been their leader for twenty years, led them on hundreds of missions to the most remote, fertile corners of the Sea. But Chuck was getting soft, and he was wrong about this one.

"Aight, man, your choice," said Zeke, who watched Banshee finger herself.

Chuck turned his head.

Wham!

Zeke sucker-punched him. Chuck's pack was torn from his back; blood poured from behind his ear. Zeke swam forward, launched a flying knee to the ribs, grabbed him behind the head, put him in the Muay Thai Plumb. Chuck ate knees for a good minute, crumpling up in a ball, unconscious. Zeke moved to the mount position, raining twelve-six elbows, head butts to his skull, until Chuck's body had been pulverized.

Zeke stepped aside. Other Diver Neurons jumped in, stomping on their venerable leader. Fractured in every way possible, Chuck was dead, his body floating belly-up toward the surface of the Sea.

After the savagery was complete, the twenty billion neurons made the trek over to Banshee. Zeke was first. He pushed her to her back, held her by the throat and pried open her legs with his free dendrite. "Time for daddy," he said, thrusting his manhood into Banshee as far as it would go. Banshee feigned resistance, as if she were being raped, yet only seconds into the intercourse, a dark red orgasm emanated from between her legs. Banshee screamed in ecstasy.

"Yes, daddy. You're so big. More, more! Harder!"

Like an iceberg had melted, a global warming of the psyche, the Sky grew dark and the seas began to rise. Rise from the testosterone of Zeke and the orgasm of Banshee. Rise from the billions of other Diver Neurons who were waiting in line to ride the train.

29 – Martin Paddles Home

Marguerite exited Martin's car and disappeared into the rain. Or maybe she jumped into the surrounding lake. Morning was upon Martin, and the car was flooded inside. Water rose to the door handles, up to his neck; driving would be impossible. The entire city of Denver became one big body of water, an entire flood plain; the only way to travel at this point would be by boat.

Martin located a canoe that was moored along the side of the basketball court. He hopped in and started paddling through the streets of Denver, through the storm of the century that unleashed rain at a rate of an inch per hour. Unprecedented in their origin and scope, meteorologists would later say the rain came from an El Nino-based disturbance in the Pacific Ocean, from Hawaii specifically, where a hurricane had formed off the coast of the Big Island, not far from where Martin and Ana got married.

Paddling west on Colfax, past Hot Chick a Latte Coffee House, Martin followed a current up Colorado Boulevard, then took a left on 23rd, where he drifted across the ninth green at the City Park Golf Course to the west side of the Denver Zoo. Except for sea lions barking in the distance, Denver was eerily quiet, almost lifeless, as Martin took a right on Walnut. Now paddling by Visions West Gallery, Martin glided by a bunch of old frames floating in the water and a portrait of Basquiat that had survived the pounding storm.

Questions came rushing in. Did Ana know about the storm? What would he tell her when she got home later today? Was she aware that Martin's cell phone went missing, that the phone lines in Denver were down, that no technology could help, that her home had been destroyed by the psychic weakness of her husband?

Martin paddled to the front door of his condo, which was three-quarters submerged in dirty water. Holding his breath, he ducked his head under and swam through the door. Inside, Martin's belongings floated around in complete disarray. A popcorn maker, bottles, lamp, shoes, photographs stuck to the sliding glass door. Martin swam through each room of his house, breast-stroking through hallways, under arches, around the office, dining room and kitchen. The entire place was chaotic, shaken, thrown around by the storm.

Martin entered his bedroom on the second level. Oddly enough, Ana's belongings were nowhere to be found. Her clothes, shoes, jewelry were gone, washed away by the rains. Martin felt wildly alone with his thoughts. Soaked, drenched, wasted inside, he wondered how this could happen. How could a storm be so devastating, take away everything Ana owned? To be clear, Martin wanted a release from suffering, perhaps even an extinguishing of the self, but this was another animal. *This* was the very fabric of suffering itself, the stuff of living nightmares, of inconsolable pain, of a one-way ticket to prison, hand-delivered by the creator of pain and suffering itself, whatever that might be. Call it God. Call it Satan. Call it gin-soaked lies cooked over Polish bacon.

Ding-dong. Pizza's here.

Martin's father gestured for his young son to answer the door.

"Go get me that dollar and a quarter tucked in folds of the couch."

"Go get me that ashtray so Mom don't go south."

"Go get me that light. Go get me that match. Go get me them basketball shoes right next to the trash."

30 – Nate's Goodbye

From a remote part of Martin's brain stem, just at the intersection of his temporal lobe, where the past and present are blurred, where the conceptual and the empirical fall away, where the self and non-self are one, where good and bad dissolve into a nebulous fluid, Nate gazed into the heart of the Storm. Circling the kitchen to get a better view, he took aerial photographs and audio of the snarling beast as it shook the household. Pictures fell from the walls. Pots and pans rattled. Hail collected on the floor below. Mothers and fathers scrambled from room to room, unnerved, praying the nightmare would come to an end.

Because *this* nightmare was different.

This storm had a new kind of intensity.

Like it could blow the walls off their house at a moment's notice. Like there could be no *a priori* assurances they would make it through the night. All they had was their faith and powers of distraction.

But Nate was different. Nate was not a man of faith or distraction. When the world seemed chaotic and uncertain, his focus became still, his senses heightened. Instead of fleeing from uncertainty, Nate wanted to stare uncertainty in the face and examine the back of its head. Sure, he was concerned that the Storm or the Sea could send him into oblivion, make all his aspirations seem childish and ignorant, but the spirit of exploration felt singular, self-justifying, an end to pursue for its own sake.

Two AM. Nate shuffled from room to room to get a better view of the turbulent cell. Settling in the kitchen, he grabbed a bottle of Windex from the cupboard and sprayed a section of the Plexiglas floor that was free of scratches and stress marks. *Wow, what a sight,* he thought to himself. The colors of the vortex were magnificent. Blues, purples, silvers, streaks of black. He placed his ear near the floor, listened to the winds shear the underside of his home. His mind raced. His heart beat fast.

Was it time?

Nate walked into his bedroom and grabbed his Gore-Tex backpack buried in his closet. He reached in and examined the contents: rope, fins, oatmeal, water, dive mask, oxygen, first aid kit, journal, pencil, life raft, parachute.

Yeah, it was time.

Tearing a page from his journal, Nate wrote a letter to his father:

Dear Dad,

What I'm about to say is going to be hard for you to hear, but please know I'm not making this decision lightly. This is what I've been planning for a long time, perhaps my whole life. I have decided to enter the Storm. Before you worry or shake your head in sadness, please know I will come back safe. I promise. I have a parachute, a raft and all kinds of supplies. I have studied the movements of the Storm carefully. I am prepared.

Dad, I hope you know how much I look up to you. I have watched you live your life with integrity. You follow your principles. You follow your heart. I would like to think I am doing the same—following my heart. While I'm not an explorer of scripture, I am an explorer of other things. At times, I even feel like my quest is spiritual, like maybe God has a different plan for me. I know you don't see it the way I do, but trust me when I say I need to take this journey. If I don't, I would be living a life of regret.

Dad, it hurts me to write this letter. It hurts me because it hurts you. The last thing I want to do is disappoint you. I just want to make you proud. Hopefully one day I can do that. Please know I will come back safely. I promise. I love you, Dad, and I can't wait to see you again soon.

Your son,
Nathaniel

Nate folded up the letter and placed it on the kitchen table under a pepper grinder. Resisting the urge to second-guess himself, he grabbed a circular saw from the storage area. Nate plugged it in and flipped the switch. The circular saw fired up. He set the blade on the Plexiglas and cut a circle around an area that was weak, vulnerable, in need of repair.

The insert fell to the world below.

The outside world was cold.

Nate secured his backpack, tightened his boots and let his legs dangle from the hole. To honor Pastor Samuel, he said a quick prayer, his first genuine one in years. Nate maneuvered his body so it faced the outside of the hole. He inched himself down to his stomach, then to his elbows. *The moment was now.*

Whoosh.

He let go.

Nate disappeared into the clouds at the edge of the unknown.

31 – The Separation

Ankle-deep in water, Barrantine listened to Ana's message on his answering machine:

"I hope your office survived the storm. I want to thank you for what you have done for me, for us. I'm sure you heard; Martin and I decided to call it quits. I appreciate your efforts, but unfortunately, they proved too late. I would like to cancel my 4:00 appointment. Martin and I are finished with counseling. I also wanted to let you know that the One-Sentence Time Machine was destroyed by the water. I'm sorry for this. I do think it was working, and I would like to reimburse you for it. It's a useful device."

Barrantine set down his phone gently.

What could have gone wrong in a single day, he wondered? Certainly, Martin suffered from inner turmoil, and the destabilizing effects of counseling could never be discounted, but by all outward appearances, the counseling was going according to plan. Martin and Ana seemed like a relatively normal couple who were just working through basic challenges. Over the next couple months, he envisioned their relationship deepening, growing, moving to higher ground.

Shaking his head in disappointment, Barrantine paced around his office and placed buckets under the leaks in the roof.

Drip.

Drip.

Drip.

He peered through his window. The rain came down hard, strangely hard, trickling down walls, exploiting weaknesses in the building's structure, finding any vulnerabilities overlooked by the building's designer.

Designer.

The word pooled in Barrantine's brain. Did Mother Nature want to be heard, through the clouds and the rain and the suffocating gusts of wind? Though Barrantine tried to avoid superstition, he couldn't help but wonder if Mother Nature was responding to her inhabitants, sending them messages about the consequences of their actions, how they fit into a greater scheme. Though she was forceful and indirect in her communication, perhaps she needed to speak in these ways, so her moral subordinates could feel her emotion.

Barrantine pulled wet papers from his desk drawer, draped them over the arms of his swiveling leather chair. Careful not to touch the papers, he sat down and made notes on the inside cover of Spinoza's *Ethics.* "We are all part of a greater whole," he wrote. "Grains of sand on an infinite beach. Birds flying in alignment. But none of the birds see the alignment, none of the grains of sand know it is a beach."

Barrantine's pencil broke in half. He tossed it across the room.

Where is Martin?

32 – Nate's Descent

Poof. Nate's parachute deployed in the middle of the Storm. His momentum slowed down. The trajectory of his fall stabilized. It worked! He wiped his goggles to get a better view of the frothy auburn clouds flashing light and dark from lightning strikes. What a beautiful sight. Nate grabbed his camera from a side pocket on his backpack, tried to focus the lens. The centrifugal force threw him to the outermost part of the vortex. Loud ripping gusts of wind sheared his parachute. His ears rang. Ice formed over his lips and two-day stubble. And at that moment, Nate felt the fragility of his own existence, his fate frozen in time by the mood of the Storm.

But as panic took hold, the Storm died down and a slice of blue sky appeared. Nate leaned into the light. Pop! He broke through the outer wall. The sun shined on his face. Falling now felt tranquil, calm, easy, as if he were in a dream. Each time he pulled on one of the parachute cords, his cellular body moved in the intended way. Each time he glanced at his watch, a minute passed like an hour. Reality itself seemed elusive, warped, divided by forces beyond his comprehension.

Nate snagged his snorkeling set and secured it around his neck. He checked to make sure his inflatable boat would deploy when it hit the surface. The world below became large, imminent, ready to explode. Until there it was.

The Sea broke through the mist.

Dove-white sea caps crumbled along her surface.

Swells lifted and fell.

Nate looked at his watch. By his calculations, he would hit the water in 120 seconds...100 seconds...90 seconds...60 seconds...30 seconds. Now 10 seconds away from one of the great mysteries of existence.

33 – Martin's Job

Martin began reassembling the contents of his house. Books. Chairs. Clothes, which he hung out to dry on his porch. In his pocket, he found the One-Sentence Time Machine.

"Fuck," he said to himself, and pushed the button.

Nothing seemed to happen. But "fuck" was only a word, not a sentence. "Fuck this time travel shit," he said, and pushed the button. Again nothing happened. By all appearances, the sentence remained in reality just like all the other stupid shit he did in his life. The device was shot. He tilted it upside down. Water dripped from the edges of the bezel.

Martin changed into dry clothes, put on rain gear and started paddling north to Front Range Community College. Now catching a westerly current along I-70, he paddled up Sheridan to 112th Ave., finally mooring his boat at the main entrance to the college. He peered through a window. All the offices were closed. Only construction workers could be seen trying to clean up the mess. Martin walked into the kitchen. A foot of water had pooled on the floor.

His boss stepped out of the shadows.

"Oh, hi," said Martin.

His boss did not respond.

"This is terrible. I didn't think the rains would be so heavy this far north."

"It's wasn't just the rains," said his boss.

"What?"

"Whoever worked the closing shift on Friday left the water running. From what I could gather, the person who mopped the floor forgot to shut off the spigot. Because it was over the weekend, and with all the rain, security didn't notice. They were busy tending to other matters. Water has been pouring over the mop bucket for four days straight. We are gonna be closed for quite a while."

Martin's boss pointed to the work schedule tacked up to a corkboard. "Weren't you the one who closed on Friday?"

Martin stared at his feet, which were submerged in water. Feeling like a statue of pain, he tried to recall exactly what happened on Friday. He was in a hurry to wrap up work before his appointment with Barrantine. He wanted to leave early so he could grab a beer. Marguerite had been texting him throughout the day. He was restless, distracted, pulled out of the present moment by illicit thoughts. *This* was the night.

"Yeah, it was me," he said, shaking his head. "I guess I should probably leave now."

Martin turned away from his boss, left the kitchen and stepped into the falling rain. Standing in front of his canoe, he watched a seagull land in the flood waters. A memory surfaced from when Martin was twelve years old, living on the west side of Seattle. His dad had flown in from Denver to watch his basketball game that night. Martin was excited, wanted to put on a show for his dad, be a positive force in his parents' life. If he played well, his parents might be inspired to rekindle their love.

Martin goes baseline, hits a jumper!

Martin drives to the hoop, gets fouled and sinks the shot!

Martin jukes left, steps back, hits an Allen Iverson three!

But Martin barely registered a blip on the stat sheet, 0-4 from the field and three turnovers. And Dad only attended half the game. Said he had a meeting he couldn't miss. Said he was tired. Said he needed to make Martin's mom happy. Later, heavy drinking ruled the night. A fight broke out. Screaming, hollering, nasty words. Martin heard his name a couple times, imagined he was a part of the problem. His poor showing on the court didn't help. Bursting into tears, he flew out of his house, straight down 80th to Golden Gardens Park.

Martin slammed into the sea, touched the sandy bottom with his fingers, stayed under until he couldn't hold his breath. When he surfaced, he had been transported to a better place. To his imagination. To the multi-tiered constructs a twelve-year-old builds in the recesses of his own mind where reality is spun differently. New narratives are born. New plot lines develop. New layers are added to the existing subfloor to hold it together, keep it strong. Epoxy. Acrylic. Clear plastic laminate to keep out water.

Martin bent over, picked up the paddle on his canoe and watched a seagull wet its beak in the salty Denver brine. Oh, what it would be like to be a bird, to fly without regret, land wherever it pleases. There's no gluttony or negligence in bird's life. No regret. No days spent reflecting on beginnings and endings. When a bird eats or drinks, it eats or drinks. When a bird lands in water, it simply lands in water.

34 – Nate Finds the Sea

Splash! Nate plunged into the emerald green water. After holding his breath for a full minute, his head popped up. He scanned the surface of the Sea, tried to get his bearings. One by one, long, heavy waves rolled by, pulling him into their troughs, pushing him over the crests like a piece of driftwood. Nate thrashed around. He swallowed gulps of ocean water and coughed. Disgusting, he thought to himself. *The Sea tastes like shit.*

Now treading water, Nate tried to relax, take stock of the situation. Did he still have his backpack? Yep, on his back. What about the collapsible oar? Got it. And the life raft? Where did the life raft go? Nate's breathing grew shallow as he realized it had come dislodged from his backpack. His head moved on a swivel. Panic ensued. Okay, there it was only a few feet away. He swam over to the life raft, located the valve and turned it counterclockwise. The circular rubber tube inflated.

Nate lifted himself into the boat. His throat was dry. Where was the drinking water? Right there, attached to the side of his pack with a carabiner. He guzzled water from his bottle. Much better. What's next? The parachute. Who knows if he might need it again? Nate pulled the lines in and stuffed the parachute in a bag.

One by one, waves continued to roll by, lifting Nate to the heavens, dropping him back down into the depths of the Sea. Something about the repetitive cadence left him feeling helpless, alone. He needed to get control of the situation. Time to start moving. Nate unfolded the collapsible oar from the side of his pack and started to paddle. But to where? There were no landmarks, nothing distinct to paddle toward. The Sea felt immense, bottomless, uncontained, like it went on forever.

Breathing deeply, Nate tried to find a rhythm with his paddling. Five strokes on the right side, five strokes on the left. Again. Five strokes on the right side, five strokes on the left. Slowly but surely, the life raft started to cut through the waves, and Nate grew more comfortable. Yet after only an hour, his stomach began to gurgle. His face turned green. Nausea took hold. Nate leaned over the side of the boat and heaved.

He heaved again.

And again.

Nate vomited eight more times over the course of several hours until his stomach felt like it had been ravaged by piranhas. Exhausted, he laid back, fixated on the Sky. The moon glowed. Stars glistened above. Where had the day gone? Had three hours passed or ten? And the Sea? She was darker, colder, saltier, than he anticipated. And the sickness was worrisome. But at least there was no sign of evil sea witches, no long-clawed beasts hunting him down for a meal.

35 – Back in Counseling

For the first time in two weeks, the sky started to lighten, and the heavy rains that flooded Denver turned into a light drizzle. With only a few inches of water on the streets, the city began to gather itself. Homes began to dry. Gutters were washed clean of debris. Boats were moored. Life jackets put away. There was even a sense that all the rain was good for the Front Range. Perhaps the soil and the grass and the trees needed the water. Mother Nature always had a silver lining, a greater purpose for her outpourings.

Martin unzipped his rain jacket and sat on the couch next to Mazzy, who was curled up in a ball.

"Thank you for seeing me on such short notice. I'm sorry to come back under these conditions. What a mess with all the rain."

Barrantine ran his hand across his beard. "I'm just glad that you *did* come back. Regardless of what else happened, I think it's important to process these events, to learn and grow." Barrantine reviewed his notes. "So, I realize this is difficult to talk about, but what happened with you and Ana? The last time I saw you, your relationship appeared to be moving in a positive direction."

Martin swallowed hard. "Yeah, maybe I wasn't as honest as I could have been during that last session. Maybe I have more issues than I care to admit. Anyway, I cheated on Ana. I got drunk and I cheated on her."

"With who?"

"With the woman who I've been texting, Marguerite."

"I see, and was this the first time you've been with Marguerite?"

"Basically."

"What do you mean?"

"I guess I had sort of crossed some lines before, but not to this extent."

"Do you care for this other woman?"

"No, not at all. I have no interest in Marguerite, none. I lost perspective and made a stupid decision. I feel like a total piece of shit."

"And the One-Sentence Time Machine? Were you using it at the time?"

Martin pulled the watch from his pocket. "It's broken, actually. It got wet in all the rain. I'm sorry. It helped, but I probably relied too heavily on it."

"How so?"

"I think erasing my words came too easy," said Martin, "and more words tended to come out. And then my impulsivity kind of took over."

"I see," said Barrantine, "and was your impulsivity the root cause of this episode with Marguerite?"

"Possibly."

"Your honesty is notable, Martin. A couple more questions. Would you say that you fantasize about other women frequently? Do you fantasize even when you are with Ana?"

"On occasion, yes."

Barrantine circled an entire paragraph in his notes.

"So, before we go any further, I would like to note that much of this is quite normal. The number of times people have sexual thoughts during a single day is frequent, perhaps in the hundreds for men, if you believe the studies." Barrantine cleared his throat. "However, I do believe hypersexuality is a consideration here. Are you familiar with this term?"

"I've heard it before, yes."

"Good. The name sort of says it all. Hypersexuality is basically a condition in which a person is consumed with sexual thoughts, and the key is that this consumption often has deleterious effects on one's life. Now, I am not saying you have this condition per se, but there is a scale, right? Hypersexuality is not a black and white diagnosis."

Martin began petting Mazzy. "Is it genetic?"

"Good question." Barrantine opened up an anatomy book sitting on the corner of his desk. "Let's talk brain structure for a second. Here's the amygdala. Here's the hippocampus and the limbic node. A lot of our sexual desires occur in these areas, specifically where dopamine is processed in the mesolimbic pathway. However, even though our sexual regulatory center has a biological origin, this does not mean it was genetically determined. Life experiences also come into play."

"Like upbringing?" asked Martin. "Like the stuff with my parents?"

"That's a common one, and in your case, it's a strong consideration, but it could be past experiences with a friend or girlfriend. Basically, anything that involves suffering. Hypersexuality, or any addiction really, if we want to use that word, is often an adaptive response to the inner pain from one's past, or to the post-traumatic effects of suffering itself. From a clinical standpoint, then, it becomes necessary to understand one's past pain, and to redirect and channel it."

"Channel?"

"Yes, as in, find new outlets for our impulses. In short, lifestyle changes are needed, to influence the underlying brain chemistry, creating new neural connections that help with self-regulation. If we do not find ways to influence the internal world of our psyches, the pressure can make us act out of character, which might have been what happened with you."

"Makes sense," said Martin. "Thank you."

"Of course, you are welcome." Barrantine glanced at his watch. "Now, I know I did a lot of the talking today, and for that I apologize. But hopefully our conversation will help lay the foundation for our future sessions. Going forward, my hope is that we can clarify what is going on deep inside, so we can translate these unconscious neural happenings into words or images. For now, I would like the focus to be solely on you. Later we can discuss what this means in the context of your relationship with Ana."

36 – Ana's Anxiety

Since the separation, Ana had been staying at her friend Marie's house. Although the arrangement provided a solid distraction and was even a little healing that first week, Ana's mood had taken a downward turn over the last few days. Her vision narrowed, confidence weakened, desperate feelings started to intervene, especially in the mornings when Marie had already left for work and the house was empty. Silence was the only thing on offer. Unstable silence. The kind that lives in a waiting room after a doctor detects a suspicious growth. Tests are run. Life is put on hold. All you can do is remain.

Ana hadn't felt this unstable since her father's death. At the time, she suffered from debilitating panic attacks and prolonged bouts of loneliness. Hard-charging questions surged forward, questions that were never fully addressed until Martin had entered her life. Who would watch over her when she was depressed? What if she needed to move a couch or fix a leaky pipe or blow leaves from her gutters? Who could she consult when her job became compromising, when the walls in her house felt like they were closing in?

Ana's fingers tingled. Her pulse elevated. Sweat dripped from her palms. All the symptoms came without warning, charging forward like a bison galloping across a field. Until one day the symptoms became predictable, and she could see the bison start to kick up dust; fear was on the horizon, a sense of being close to a cliff's edge, about to step off.

She sat up in her bed. A knot twisted in her stomach. Her chest tightened. She hadn't slept, and the prospect of work felt dungeonesque. All signs pointed to a new wave of anxiety, a sense of not being anchored to this world and needing help. Ana rummaged through an old bag of toiletries. A Xanax prescription from five years ago was tucked into one of the pockets. Did Xanax work after five years? Even if it was half effective, it would be better than nothing, and she could always double the dose. Ana poured herself a glass of water and swallowed the pill. In minutes, the edge smoothed over; the bison laid in the grass.

Now sifting through a box of mementos she grabbed from the condo, Ana cracked open her high school yearbook. East High School: Class of 2000. She paged through the book until she found a picture of herself playing the clarinet in the band. Ana tossed the yearbook aside, shuffled through old pictures. A photo of her mother and father standing beside a Christmas tree. Another of her father placing wrapping paper in the fire, red glints of light shooting from the sides of his glasses.

Ana walked over to the window. The skies were grey. Clouds pinched down on the trees. Light rain tore as it fell. She reached into the closet, grabbed an umbrella. When was the last time she felt such an intense need for protection from the rain? When was the last time she needed it to stop so badly? Her wedding, she supposed, in the anxious hours before the ceremony, when she would forever place her trust in Martin's hands.

And now this.

How could Martin be so selfish, so oblivious, so ungrateful, knowing that trust was Ana's Achilles heel? She'd done a lot for him over the years, helped him with all kinds of things. Buying his first home. Getting out of credit card debt. Staying organized at work. Martin didn't even know how to populate a cell on an Excel spreadsheet before meeting her. And what about the loving notes she left around the house when Martin was going through difficult times with his parents? And the long conversations about boundary setting, about using Martin's past experiences as motivation to better himself?

Ana had structured her entire life around Martin. She'd embraced him during the best of times, leaned on him during the worst.

Now her dignity was gone, confidence pulled from inside her chest, thrown against the wall, bruised, cracked, exploited, undermined, laid bare for the entire world to see. What should she do now, or a year from now? Could she forgive? Really forgive? Or half forgive, forced by her own sense of powerlessness, her own drifting through the air like a worn-out plastic bag, unsure where she would fall.

On a street.

In a tree.

On a branch that might tear her at the seam.

Marie knocked on the door.

"Come in," said Ana, previously unaware that Marie was home.

"I forgot my computer," said Marie, watching a tear run down Ana's cheek. Marie ignored the tear. She needed to be strong for Ana, to show her everything was fine and that her life had not been turned upside down. Ana wasn't crying. She just had a piece of lint in her eye.

"Do you want to carpool today?" asked Marie. "I could drop you off at work and pick you up. We can do happy hour and dinner."

"Thanks for the thought," said Ana. "But I have a meeting at Lowry today, so I'll need my car."

"All right, honey, but text me about happy hour. It will be fun. We can make plans for the weekend." Marie placed her hand on Ana's shoulder. "You look beautiful today, by the way. You know that, don't you? I love the yellow sweater."

"Thanks," said Ana, lowering her head. "I'll text you later."

When Marie left the room, Ana dropped her umbrella, took off her coat and fell to the bed. She buried her head in a pillow and sobbed uncontrollably. Unable to gather herself enough to make it to work on time, Ana picked up the phone and told her boss she would be late.

"My roof is still leaking," she said, "and I'm going to have to call a roofer to come fix it."

Drip.

Drip.

Drip.

"Puddles are everywhere," she continued. "This might take a while to clean up."

37 – *The Darkness in our Lives*

"I'd like to talk about the darkness in our lives, all of our lives," said Barrantine, "the darkness that has been spoken of for who-knows-how-long. Now, Freud associated it with our id. Carl Jung referred to it as our shadow. Nietzsche, I think, viewed it as much more biological. I tend to believe Nietzsche was closest, yet perhaps the Jungian language of shadows is most helpful."

Barrantine stroked his beard.

"Martin, we left off last time discussing the events that led up to your separation from Ana, and we discussed the possibility that such events had a hypersexual origin. Further, we discussed how these sexual impulses originate in our unconscious grey matter and speak their own neurophysiological language, where said impulses take on a hidden, inaccessible quality that is both causally powerful and compromising. We also considered how this might be anchored in the unique challenges that you had experienced during your upbringing. Are we tracking together?"

Martin smiled at Barrantine's heady diagnosis. "I think so."

"Very good. To continue, then, I'd like to ask you a question. On the night when you met this other woman, can you describe what you were feeling inside? Do any images come to mind?"

Martin touched his hairline. "Maybe a runaway train driven by a blind engineer."

"Ha, yes, very good. An apt description for the unconscious in general. I especially like the power it conveys, and the sense that it should not be taken lightly and can take on a life of its own if one is not careful. This is indeed a very Jungian perspective, particularly when it comes to this idea that archetypes, even entire stories or myths, can live inside us unconsciously." Barrantine made notes in his journal. "Let's go back to the image of a runaway train. What should one do with it, besides trying to control its momentum? There needs to be a plan, right? A plan that anticipates and prevents the train from losing its brakes."

"And it would probably help to have an engineer who can see," added Martin.

"Indeed. And what does it mean for an engineer to see? Any thoughts on this?"

"Maybe just being aware of the triggers. Like, being aware of what causes the sexual impulses in the first place."

"An astute observation," said Barrantine. "And what do you think triggered you that night?"

"I honestly don't know. I was at work, then I came here for my appointment. The conversation about my mother might have caught me off guard...especially the bizarre stuff with the underwear."

"Yes, the whole episode had to be unsettling."

"Oh, and I was also texting Marguerite."

Barrantine recalled Martin's phone buzzing during their last session.

"So, you were using the internet during work. Is it fair to say that you were distracting yourself?"

"Yeah, that's fair."

"From your job?"

"I'm probably a little burned-out."

"And would you say this burnout is fleeting? Or are you unsatisfied in a more lasting way?"

Martin felt like he was being cross-examined. "I'm probably a little tired of my job period."

"I see. This could be a significant piece of the puzzle. I recall that you said that cooking played an important part of your life, as it pulled you out of your difficult situation with your mother?"

"I was basically kicked out of my house, and cooking helped me survive."

"Survive your mother?"

"Definitely."

"And would you say it brought you closer to your father?"

"What do you mean?"

"I guess I'm just referring to your desire to move in with him when you were a young boy. I recall your father was in the restaurant business. Perhaps cooking helped you feel closer to him?"

Martin was silent for several seconds. "I don't know. I've never thought about that before."

Barrantine began sketching cooking items. Pots and pans. A colander. Yellow bell peppers. Mozzarella cheese. Bacon bits. Red pepper flakes. "And why did your mom kick you out of the house?"

"I didn't get along well with her third husband."

"I see. Now, to me, that sounds like cooking is an outlet for your shadow—a shadow forged by your relationship with both parents. Would you agree?"

"It was definitely a survival issue, and it is one of my passions."

"Indeed," said Barrantine. "In my opinion, being a chef is like being an artist, and artists are in the business of harnessing their shadows and translating them into sounds or words or images or tastes. When a person's outer life, which is to say, one's consciousness, is out of sync with one's dark side, that's when problems can occur. In this way, the artist might go off the rails and not channel his or her shadow in a productive way, which can lead to all kinds of regrettable results." Barrantine pictured Rothko and Bourdain. "I do believe this dynamic is worth considering here. In other words, are your passions being realized in your life in the right way? If they are not, then has your shadow grown darker, more pronounced, with a bigger penumbra that is encroaching on other parts of the brain?"

38 – Banshee's Wail

Just at the anterior lobe of Martin's pituitary gland, where waves of corticotropin hormones were being prepped and distributed along his adrenal cortex, Zeke swam as the leader of the Diver Neurons for the first time. After satiating his nature in the most fundamental ways, he initially felt calm, relaxed, powerful. Now that Chuck was gone and Desmond had been relegated to bitch status, Zeke could set the tone for the Diver Neurons, take them any old place he wanted. No need to discriminate when it came to sex. Fat, skinny, short or tall. Dark sex. Light sex. Sex is sex. Any old ho will do.

But only ten days after going balls deep in Banshee, Zeke and the rest of the Diver Neurons were taken aback by the dark, empty feeling of the Sea. Fewer mermaids. Genderless creatures were everywhere, as were creatures who arguably had no sex whatsoever, or had sex where the females dominated. Seahorses, for example. When seahorses copulated, the female simply deposited her eggs in a cute little pouch on the abdomen of the male. There was no ass slapping. No dirty talk, rape simulation or the like. Arguably, there wasn't any real penetration at all. Or if there was, the female seahorses were the ones running the show, which was gay as hell.

On top of it all, the seas were now warm to the touch, which caused water levels to rise even more. And a wailing, piercing scream emanated through the water, hurting the ears of the Diver Neurons, bringing on a sense of anxiety and existential angst that, when paired with the burning sensation on the tip of their penises, proved discouraging. Red, inflamed, oozing with yellow discharge, a good two-thirds of the Diver Neurons had come down with a case of the clap, making it hurt to pee, hurt to swim, hurt to even talk or think about. As such, their libidos had been greatly diminished, and they didn't feel like themselves.

But they kept swimming, kept searching for a sea change, hoping the clap would go away and the wails would stop so they could regain their sense of self. For ten days, they swam through warming seas and cloudy waters, bodies sluggish, egos weak and indistinguishable, penises scorching like magma.

Now circling back to the cave where they first saw Banshee, Zeke decided they needed to confront the bow-legged slut about her sexual health. Was Banshee aware she carried an STD? Did she realize the sea had warmed? Could she hear the loud screams? Little did the Diver Neurons know, Banshee was not only aware of it all, she was the cause and was pleased as punch about the whole thing.

When they arrived at the copulation site, Banshee was sprawled out on a ledge overlooking a hydrothermal vent, howling like a wolf.

Zeke announced himself through the hazy water. "Where you at?"

Banshee stopped howling. "You stupid creatures," she said, now speaking English.

Zeke's mouth flopped open. Why hadn't Banshee spoken English before?

"You mindless little faggots," she continued.

As the Diver Neurons swam closer to Banshee, they noticed her appearance had changed. No longer the pantiless freak they had diddled two weeks prior, her makeup ran down her cheeks. Her hair was disheveled. Banshee's eyes were dark and sunken-in like she'd been freebasing coke for a week. Though her ass still had appeal, the Diver Neurons noted it resembled a giant plate of cottage cheese you could get lost in for days. And underneath her torn, dirty jeans, the orange sponge had gone into hiding. Like it had been locked down in a vice-grip, Banshee's pussy appeared nonexistent, put away for good.

39 – Ana's Shadow

Ana picked up the phone and called Dr. Barrantine.

"Hello," said Barrantine.

"Hi, it's Ana. Ana, from counseling, Martin's wife."

"Ana, yes, of course, nice to hear your voice."

"Say, do you mind if I come in and see you. I know I said I was done with counseling, but I thought it might be good for me to talk to a professional."

"Sure, of course," said Barrantine. "Do you want to come in later this week?"

"Actually, I was hoping I could come in today."

"Today, hmmm...what time?"

"How about now?"

Barrantine examined his calendar.

"I did have a cancellation after lunch, which I guess is right now. Sure, come on over."

Ana arrived fifteen minutes later. She sat down on the brown tweed couch. Barrantine could see the tension in her being.

"Talk to me," said Barrantine. "What is going on?"

"Well, as I mentioned on my phone message, Martin and I are no longer together. I left him because of what he did. He cheated on me. He cheated on me with the woman he was texting." Ana slapped her hands on her lap. Her voice trembled. "And I'm really pissed. I'm sad and I'm very hurt, but I'm also pissed."

Barrantine considered revealing to Ana that he'd been counseling Martin, but decided to bite his tongue.

"I'm so sorry to hear this, but you need to understand that your feelings are entirely normal and justified. Anyone in your situation would feel the same."

"Thank you. I'm sorry if I'm coming across too strong. I've been feeling very out of sorts after the separation, and I don't know if I made the right decision. I don't know if I totally gave my all to the relationship. I have also been self-medicating with an old prescription my doctors gave me years ago."

"What are you taking?"

"Xanax."

"Have you always struggled with anxiety?"

"Not always. I think I told you that right around the time my father died, I was going through hard times. That's when I started to suffer from panic attacks."

"You said your father died suddenly, correct?"

Mazzy jumped up on Ana's lap, turned in a circle and sat down. Ana bit her lower lip. "I wasn't totally honest about my father's death. He died suddenly, but he actually committed suicide."

The lighting in the room grew dim. Barrantine crossed his legs. "What happened? Why did he do it?"

"No one really knows for sure. My dad was a quiet person who held a lot in. He never really liked his job. I mean, he liked math, but he didn't like talking in front of people. Plus, he suffered from depression."

"And what was his relationship like with your mother?"

"It was good on the whole, but they were both private people. I never saw them discuss their marriage. There were times when they would quit talking to each other for days."

"I see. And so, the communication was hidden beneath the surface?"

"They both held a lot in, yes."

"Was this common?"

"Kind of. My parents were very structured."

"Can you give me an example of the type of structure you're referring to?"

"The house for one. My mother liked to keep a tidy house. Everything had its place. And both my parents had a set schedule when it came to dinner and bedtime. My dad suffered from insomnia and was quite particular about his sleep routine. He was a restless sleeper, so they slept in different rooms."

"And did this seem unusual?"

"Sleeping in different rooms?"

"Yes, and the structure, and the fact that they didn't argue?"

"Oh, most of it felt pretty normal. Or, I suppose when I got older, it started to seem a little odd. The lack of arguing especially. I think in a way my parents had kind of a '50s mentality. And maybe that's how my dad responded to his depression—by suppressing it, or pretending it wasn't there. My dad was never comfortable showing his emotions."

"Ana, that strikes me as an astute observation. And how do you think this influenced you?"

"Maybe I'm less vocal. I probably don't show my emotions as much as I should."

"In your relationship with Martin?"

"Right."

"Would you mind elaborating?"

"I can try. I suppose one issue that comes to mind is Martin's visiting certain websites. It always bothered me, but I brushed it under the carpet."

"Are you referring to pornography?"

"Yes."

"I see. Thank you for your honest responses, Ana." Barrantine began drawing in his journal. Vertical lines. A gate. A black picket fence. "Now, going back to the medication you were taking, the Xanax, did you start taking it immediately after your father's death?"

"A couple months after, yes. My counselor at the time suggested it."

"When did you stop taking it?"

Ana ran her hand along Mazzy's spine. "Shortly after I met Martin. He helped me get out of my funk. We started being really active—hiking, camping, road trips. We flew to St. Thomas in the Caribbean. He was really good for me then."

"Tell me more, Ana. In what respects was Martin helpful? Was it primarily because he took your mind off the terrible pain you were experiencing, or were there other factors?"

"I just fell in love with him, I guess. I fell in love with his personality, his cooking, his quirks. He was easy to talk to, laidback. Martin was what my parents were not, especially my father. He came across as very free and positive on the outside."

"And on the inside?"

Ana shook her head. "On the inside, I don't know. I'm probably not in the best place to discuss that right now. Obviously, I love Martin, but I've seen changes in him over the last year or so. He's been more disconnected, more distant. I think he's having a hard time coming to terms with his father."

"With his alcoholism?"

"Yes, and their relationship in general. Martin doesn't let on how much it bothers him. I think he's in pain. I think both of them are in pain. You know, his dad is actually a pretty nice man. Funny, has a ton of charisma, or at least used to. It's where Martin gets his personality."

"I take it you've spent time with Martin's father?"

"Yes, years ago before the alcoholism had taken its toll. Alonzo is his name. He used to come over to the house on occasion. He'd even bring me flowers and write funny notes. I sorta got the feeling he was trying for make up for past mistakes. But Martin never seemed to want to forgive."

"Forgive the alcoholism?"

"That, and his childhood in general. I think he feels like Alonzo abandoned him. And now that Alonzo is ill, Martin doesn't know what to do with it."

"I see," said Barrantine. "Thank you for providing this background. I think it's helpful when it comes to grasping the bigger picture."

"Of course, but right now, none of that matters. Right now, I feel like Martin stabbed me in the heart and twisted the blade. I feel really weak and pathetic. And it's affecting my living situation, my sleep, my job. Nothing feels right. So I'm hoping to get to a better place."

"Sure, of course, Ana. I think you made a wise choice. I'm happy you came back to see me. I think it's safe to say that Mazzy feels the same."

40 – Barrantine's Discovery

Barrantine dimmed the lights and sat down at his desk. Although he felt good about his progress with Ana, a nagging feeling brewed inside, a sense of self-doubt, perhaps even fraudulence, about the direction of his own practice. Barrantine had always advertised himself as an experimental philosophical counselor, yet lately, all he seemed to be doing was talking, analyzing, asking his clients questions about childhood. At the end of the day, Barrantine wondered if he was really anything more than a cognitive or psychoanalytic therapist.

The main housing unit for the One-Sentence Time Machine in front of him, Barrantine blew dust away and loosened six screws on the motherboard. His mind turning like the gears in a Rolex watch, he grabbed old journals from his desk drawer and read from a May 11, 1981, entry. He was twenty-seven years old at the time. The theoretical foundations of artificial intelligence were foremost on his mind. Turing. Wittgenstein. The truth-functional nature of language. Symbolized words that were represented by truth tables and downloaded on the hardware of the machine, where they could later interface with consciousness and the quantum world.

That was the theory anyway. In practice, the machine proved far more complicated. Twenty years of tinkering before a fraction of time could be reversed. *Twenty years.* And for what? For single sentences? At the time, Barrantine's invention felt profound, revolutionary, the stuff of genius. Single sentences *do* make a difference in our lives. But now the technology seemed dated, and Barrantine worried he had hung his hat on it for too long. Perhaps it was time to create a new program, a version capable of transcending the grammatical confines of our experience, moving past words, as it were, past cognitive representations, past the everyday lightness of being.

Tossing his journal aside, Barrantine connected a microphone to the machine and placed a headset over his ears. Next, he pulled wires from the command center and rerouted them to different parts of his own body—his head, wrist, armpits. Basically, any part of his person that helped deliver emotions was connected to the outputs of the machine. Now fully interfaced to the device, he started uttering obscure sounds. Grunts, groans, humming, singing, chanting. Feelings of impatience, anger, joy and deviance poured from his mouth.

The machine started to light up.

Sensing the momentum, Barrantine entered his computer and started searching for porn. Given that sex so often lies at the root of our unconscious psyche, and having seen endless couples come into his practice with sexual issues, Barrantine sought the dirtiest images possible, pictures with the potential to make his heart pound with forbidden pleasure. To be clear, Barrantine was not a porn guy, and he wasn't doing this for fun or escape. No, he was doing it in the name of research, in the pure pursuit of science and philosophy, a selfless plunge into the soot and sundry of the unconscious. In short, Barrantine was trying to give rise to feelings in himself that the machine could one day erase.

A licentious murk hovering over his thoughts, he clicked play on a video called *Step Daddy Needs Help in the Shower*. Step Daddy had a broken arm and a cast covered with plastic. Step Daddy needed Step Daughter to help wash himself, to hand him the towel and such. Although he found the scene disturbing and repulsive, Barrantine's libido flared up like a welder's arc, and the machine sparkled in places it never had before, eventually morphing into a beautiful kaleidoscope of color when Step Daughter started to wash Step Daddy below the waist.

While *Step Daddy Needs Help in the Shower* continued to play, Barrantine knew it was time to act. Just as Step Daughter had moved to her knees, Barrantine placed the time machine watch on his wrist. Deeply focused on the motion of Step Daughter's hands as she washed Step Daddy, Barrantine's manhood, which was indeed attached to one of the wires under the table, started to rise, as did his impulse to be Step Daddy.

Barrantine pushed the button on the watch.

The impulse to be Step Daddy went away.

And so did the strength of his manhood.

But Step Daughter now washed Step Daddy to the fullest extent, and the impulse to be Step Daddy reoccurred, only this time it packed a bigger punch. Barrantine pushed the button. Again the impulse went away. He repeated the sequence. Sure enough, the sexual urge disappeared. Even when new porn was introduced to the experiment, the same outcome happened without fail. No matter how strong the desire, no matter how powerful the need for sexual completion felt, the device had successfully kicked the old impulses to the curb, sending them to an alternate world where time-scraps of old porn were discarded.

Exhausted from watching sexual images for four straight hours without achieving climax, Barrantine leaned back and collapsed in his leather chair like an old pair of wadded-up G-string panties.

Part 4: The Intractable Nature of the Sea

41 – Pastor Samuel's Angst

Pastor Samuel put his hands over the hole in the Plexiglas. The air was below zero. Ice crystals formed on his fingertips. He could see his breath. Sick with worry, he sat down at the kitchen table, lifted the pepper grinder and read the letter from Nate. When he finished, Pastor Samuel swallowed hard and placed the folded-up letter in the interior pocket of his clerical robe.

"What happened, Pastor? Where's Nathaniel?" asked one of the Angel Neurons who stood around the hole.

Tears formed in the Pastor's eyes.

"He entered the Storm."

Everyone gasped. Mothers and fathers trembled in fear. Brothers and sisters wept.

"What are we going to do?" asked one of the mothers, who fixated on the lonely, uninhabitable sky, which flashed lighting strikes in all directions.

"I think we must wait," said Pastor Samuel.

"Wait for what?"

"Wait for the Storm to die down so Nate can come home." This was the first time Pastor Samuel had ever called his son Nate.

"How will he come home?" asked one of the fathers.

"I'm not sure," said Pastor Samuel, his lip quivering. "Let's just cover the hole lightly so he can push his way through. I believe my son will find his way home." Pastor Samuel's hands shook as he opened the pantry door and tore off a piece of plastic. "Brother Cornel, will you help me tape this off? Perhaps we can also place cinder blocks around the hole, along with fluorescent tape. We don't want any accidents."

Brother Cornel placed his hands on his chest. "Yes, Pastor, of course."

"Young brothers," said Brother Cornel to a group of Angel Neurons who stood in the corner of the kitchen, "can you help me and Pastor Samuel out?"

"Yes."

"Yes, of course."

The Angel Neurons quickly placed cinder blocks around the hole.

Pastor Samuel watched in a kind of grim shock, as if he was in the presence of a terminally ill patient. His expression was dull, ambiguous. Sharp lines bisected his forehead. His shoulders felt like they were weighted with anchors. Though he knew he needed to put on a good face for the younger Angel Neurons, every subatomic particle in his cellular body said no to putting on false pretenses, and for a minute the Pastor questioned not only his own faith, but the very nature of God Himself—that He was listening, that He was all-powerful and all-knowing, that He presided over the world, that He cared.

42 – The Boredom of Life

June 1st. No lyrics to the song, but the rain pattered down like a million tiny cymbals. Martin looked out his window at dusk. A sunbeam poked through the clouds on the distant horizon. He plopped down on his couch, opened his computer and started exploring different websites: ESPN, Denver Post, Rotten Tomatoes. What next? Water damage remediation. How to get rid of mold. New kitchen countertops. TV on the Radio's next album. Porn.

Although he tried to resist, the typical feeling hit him. Boredom. And in this case, regret. A feeling of not knowing what to do. A sense that today was just like yesterday. That he was a failure, a bad person, cursed by his own nature, plagued by questions about how he should spend his time. Should he join a health club? Rent a movie? Cook dinner? Call Ana and beg for forgiveness?

And the pattern repeated. Just when his life started to stabilize, become normal or mundane, his thoughts would drift. And something in his psyche, deep in his core, wanted to mix it up, bubble over, escape the reality of his own decisions, stomp on stability, routine, the everyday passage of time. Was it his shadow? Torn identity? The penumbra of upbringing?

Martin clicked into Craigslist's casual encounters and began browsing the profiles. The boredom of life, his own flawed character, faded into the background with the crackling rain. Lightning came to the forefront. Winds swirled. The mountains locked hands with the fog. The city lights of Denver smoldered and burned. And all of Martin's conscious thoughts appeared harmless, innocent, in the moment, the Zen of internet porn laying a spell over his psyche, relinquishing suffering in its totality, completely and totally.

Until it doesn't.

And the suffering comes back. And the question of what to do with the pornography drags one into a new form of suffering, the Zen of internet porn amplifying and diminishing all at once.

And then what?

Meaninglessness?

A smack down by the Problem of Evil?

Where *is* God anyway?

Does He know we are hurting on His watch, that we feel separated and are at loss for how to live? Martin closed his eyes and tried to explain the pain in his own life. Because if God was present, there would be a reason for his personality, a greater good that flows from his actions, even when they cause harm. Or that's what Martin remembered from Philosophy 101 anyway. That to resolve the Problem of Evil is to identify a compensating good for all of suffering. Personal. Global.

Here.

There.

Everywhere.

Sometimes Martin felt like he was experiencing the cumulative decisions and sensibilities of an entire family going back many generations. Their struggles with boredom. Their shadowy figures. The same Weather Region, same Storm, same explorers of the Sea, all of which he'd inherited from his mother and father, grandma and grandpa. Other times it felt like he was just an introvert dealing with the perils of being alone.

But could Martin transmogrify the shadowy figures of several generations of family into a new way of being? Could he change the trajectory of an entire family line for himself and his future children? Could he push the boulder to the top of the hill and have it not roll back down? Or if he didn't succeed, would it be cruel to subjugate his future children to the same Weather Region, the same Storm? Did any of this matter? Anything at all?

Martin browsed the thumbnails of nude Nubians with shaved vaginas.

He clicked into the profiles of Eastern European women with snowball shaped breasts.

Going deeper into Craigslist, Martin stumbled on the transsexual profiles. Even though he had no interest in being with a transsexual, their words caught his attention, made him want to connect to what they had to offer, what they had in common. Perhaps it was their quest for meaning and acceptance, their revealing of a new kind of normal from the backdrop of chaos. Whatever the case may be, the unusual narratives of the transsexual profiles kept him intrigued, soaked him up for a full hour, made him feel less alone, more reflective and knowledgeable about what binds us all together. And the feeling went down. Way down.

Drip, drip, drip.

To bedrock of his psyche.

To the wilds of the open water.

To a poem his dad wrote several years ago.

Martin found it under a bottle of tequila in his dad's kitchen. Thinking his dad wouldn't notice, he put it in his pocket, took it home, and, on occasion, would read it when the mood was right. Crude but funny in its own way, the poem made Martin's brain relax, made him wonder if his dad's words held wisdom, possibly even potential. Potential in his dad, sure, but more so in himself. Potential for creativity, for achieving greater heights. Whatever the case may be, Martin could use a change in perspective, so he reached into his kitchen drawer, unfolded the poem and started to read.

43 – Fucking When You Should

There's fucking when you should
and fucking when you shouldn't.
That's called fucking in the extreme.
And there's fucking when you shouldn't
and fucking when you should.
That's called fucking big and it's mean.
And there's fucking in the early morning
and fucking late at night.
That's called fucking when someone could find out.
And there's fucking on top, fucking from behind.
That's called fucking en route.
And at other times,
when you're just looking to relax and fuck real slow,
there's fucking on the couch and fucking in a basement,
just prior to a show.
And when all else fails,
and there ain't no fucking to be had,
there's fucking in your mind, fucking in your heart,
thinking 'bout good and bad.

44 – Nate Follows the Signs

Seas rolled. The vermillion sun peaked over the horizon. When Nate awoke, water sloshed back-and-forth, slapping his legs. The boat had taken on a few gallons of the ocean brine. He sat up, rubbed salt from his eyes and canvassed the horizon. What should he do? He grabbed a pot and began to scoop. But water wasn't the only problem. As he leaned up against the side of the boat, he could feel it sag like it had lost air. He unscrewed the valve cover, blew into it and listened. No sounds. Hopefully it was just settling. Time to start moving, find a rhythm, knock out the chill, the doubts. The Sea demanded his full attention.

Paddling in the direction of the sunrise, Nate tried to stay focused on the details. The motion of his paddle. The cadence of the sea swells. One minute at a time. One breath at a time. One pull of the oar at a time. If he let his mind wander too much, anxiety could creep in, or the Sea might feel too boundless, empty, overwhelming. A wave might catch him off guard and topple his boat. He might grow hungry, lose his energy. His life raft could spring an unrepairable leak and send him to the sea floor in a tragic display of the ocean's power.

Nate kept paddling. Kept pushing forward. Kept trying to stay focused. A streaking line of navy-blue clouds spiraled in. He followed the line as it corkscrewed through the sky, followed it to the highest point, where he imagined his father watching him with binoculars.

"I love you, Dad," Nate whispered. "Did you get my letter?"

Nate wondered how his father would react to the letter. Would it bring him hope that his son's life had a greater purpose? Would Pastor Samuel be able to connect Nate's choices to a belief in the Grand Narrative? Nate didn't see why not. After all, the Creator is said to work in mysterious ways. Life is a test, a challenge, a struggle for us to touch what we cannot see, to connect with the essential fabric, paddle on the same Sea. Though Nate did not believe in the Grand Narrative, he hoped his father could use it for inspiration. Or if not inspiration, maybe as a point of departure he could experience in relation to Nate. Unlikely as it was, perhaps Pastor Samuel himself might one day need to reject the Grand Narrative in order to be closer to his son.

In thinking about his father, Nate found an extra spark of energy that made him push harder. Still traveling in the direction of the navy-blue clouds and the vermillion sun, an hour or two passed. Only a feeling of purpose carried Nate forward, a sense of being filled by currents of meaning, interconnected breezes, movement, a sea with personality that would tell him what to do next.

And then It appeared.

It.

An animal whose back was as wide as a city block lumbered through the water. The beast circled Nate's boat causing it to spin. He tried to take stock of the situation. His mind raced as the animal panned him in all directions. A fountain of water erupted from the blowhole on the creature's head. A volcano of whiteness crashed down like an avalanche. Rock-like crumbles of water spackled the surface.

The creature continued to circle. *It* circled. A second pass. A third. Nate's boat rotated like a planet. A billion galaxies in between. He could see all of reality. Each part of the world. The dots. The connections between the dots. Black space. Light. The creature's consciousness, which made itself known by the bubbles in the sea foam that popped like a snare drum when it breached.

And when the creature stopped circling, when it swam in a new direction away from the sun, Nate knew the explosions from the blow hole of the beast were not to be ignored. He knew the foam trails were a sign that held meaning. He knew he should follow the great sperm whale for as long as he could.

45 – A New Invention

Posture firm, cheeks taut, glasses sparkling clean, Martin ran his fingers along the sides of his head and adjusted the top button on his plaid shirt. As if he had arrived at a junction, or had stumbled across a package wrapped in duct tape, his mannerisms were stiff, expression ambiguous. Unrest was the appearance. Uneasiness about what to say, what to do. The dynamic was an odd one that Barrantine noted in his journal with scribbles, swaths of colors, words scattered on the page, which he hoped to untangle at a later date.

Reliable or nebulous
Honest or deluded
Conspiring toward wholeness
Truth-tracking

Bloated by the multifarious shenanigans of his own grey matter

"Give me a second," said Barrantine, who walked over to the pencil sharpener. "I need to put a point on a couple of these."

"That's fine," said Martin.

Barrantine sat back down, knocked out a sketch of a person overlooking an expansive mesa.

"How has your week been?" asked Barrantine, wiping charcoal off his fingers.

"Oh, not too bad," said Martin. "A little up and down, but not bad. I've been thinking about our conversation from last session."

"Any insights?" asked Barrantine.

Martin thought about Craigslist. "Boredom seems to be a big part of it. I don't do well with boredom, which is where the electronics comes into play."

"Any thoughts on the particular brand of boredom you are experiencing? Any thoughts about the causes?"

"Upbringing," said Martin, matter-of-factly. "I don't think I learned healthy ways of dealing with boredom when I was young. I think I had a little too much free time on my hands."

"No clubs? No group sports?"

"Not really. Just skateboarding. I played basketball for a while, but I wasn't any good, so I quit. And my mom just said, sure, go for it. She didn't really care."

"And your father?"

"No idea. He probably didn't know."

"I see. And did this create any animosity when it came to your mother?"

"The boredom?"

"Or the fact that she simply let you quit?"

"Actually, it probably did. I think you can sense when you parents do and don't care."

Barrantine continued to write down words in his journal.

Memory
Temporal disconnectedness
Disregard

"Martin, this strikes me as a very self-aware observation. And I would agree with your assessment. It does indeed sound like your mother was a little too hands-off. Moreover, there's plenty of research supporting your contention. As with diet and exercise, our habits begin to take shape when we are young, and these habits transfer over into adulthood. And then you throw in electronic devices. Are they not unlike cruising around Seattle on your skateboard in the middle of the night?"

"The Dark Web," said Martin, with a half-smile.

"Indeed, so eventually, we need to learn to be more at home with ourselves, with the downtime and such, so that we can develop productive habits. Hobbies, for example, or having a gratifying job. If a person is consistently engulfed in the mundane, imagine how this further perpetuates the boredom problem." Barrantine shifted in his chair. "Not to change subjects, but I sense a difference in you today. You seem to be dressed up."

Martin adjusted his glasses. "I lost my job."

"Lost?"

"Yes, or you know, a mutual parting of ways...I'm job hunting."

"Sorry to hear this. When did this happen?"

"Two days ago. It kind of came out of nowhere. Time to turn over a new leaf, I guess."

Barrantine wondered if there was more to the story. "Absolutely. That's an excellent way to frame it. Yet, when you lose something of this magnitude, or choose to take it away, perhaps it's wise to add something back into the equation. Have you considered this?"

"A little bit. I did have a question I wanted to ask you."

"Of course."

"Is it possible to get another time travel watch?"

Unsure if he should reveal his latest invention, Barrantine glanced at the black box in the corner of the room. "Yes, Martin, this is possible. I have restored the One-Sentence Time Machine device and have made the watches usable again. Yet, there may be another item of interest. I wasn't necessarily prepared to introduce this today, but since we are on the subject, why not?"

"I'm all ears," said Martin.

"Okay, but this must be kept private. This is a prototype, and it's important that it stays in this room and this room only."

"For sure, it's just between us."

Barrantine walked over to the black box and extracted two watches from inside the machine.

"Martin, I have created a new technology that goes deeper than the One-Sentence Time Machine, deeper than mere words as it were. With this device, not just sentences, but entire impulses can be extracted from reality. Given that impulses give rise to sentences, I regard this invention as more fundamental, closer to the source, than the prior one. I'm calling it the One-Impulse Time Machine."

Martin's eyes grew wide as he considered the possibilities. "Are you saying *any* impulse can be taken away?"

"Yes, as far as I know."

"And the identical impulse won't return?"

"Based on my observations, no. As was the case with the One-Sentence Time Machine, when we turn back the clock on our sentences, or in this case our impulses, although the initial conditions remain fixed, the resulting impulses will often be different."

"Because of quantum mechanics?" queried Martin, with a slight chuckle.

"Yes, because of the unpredictable nature of neurons in our brain, or more accurately, the subatomic particles that make up our neurons. So, I might have an impulse to go mow the lawn, I push the button, and boom, the impulse transforms into a desire to go watch a movie instead. I have witnessed this in myself." Barrantine thought about *Step Daddy Needs Help in the Shower*.

"Do you mind if I see one?"

"The watch? Here you go."

Martin held the One-Impulse Time Machine device under a standing lamp. "Cool looking. I like the gold bezel."

"Thank you. I do believe this one is a bit more fashionable."

Martin set the watch on the arm of the couch. "Dr. Barrantine, there's a question I've been meaning to ask you for a while now."

"Yes."

"Does free will ever enter into any of this?"

"Into using the One-Impulse Time Machine?"

"Right, like earlier when I used the One-Sentence watch, there were times when I wondered if I had freely chosen to express myself in different ways. You know, like when I pushed the button, and a new sentence would come out of my mouth."

Barrantine placed his fingertips together and held them in front of his face. "An excellent question there, Martin. The long and the short of it is that free will actually does not enter in. Based on what we know from science and philosophy, I think it's fair to say that free will is an illusion, or at least the common-sense notion is. However, if we did have this mysterious faculty, I believe it would look and feel a lot like quantum indeterminism. Thus, from a practical standpoint, in terms of observation and semantics and first-person experiences, they would mimic each other, and it wouldn't make much of a difference whether we used the word 'free' or 'undetermined' to describe our sentence choices, or impulses in this case. With that said, if the original impulse did reoccur after the button is pushed, I am inclined to believe that said impulse represents a more permanent feature of the self."

Martin squinted. "Like if I had the impulse to vote Democrat, pushing the button wouldn't make me vote Republican?"

"Exactly. But, let me also say that with the more changeable impulses, particularly those that are trivial and/or might be at odds with our fundamental value structure—errant sexual impulses, for example—additional steps may be helpful when it comes to channeling the initial impulses into new ones."

"Okay..." said Martin.

"Here's what I mean. Suppose an impulse enters the fray; say, the desire to view a certain website. You would have a signal or prompt in your environment that helps provoke a different impulse. A whoopee cushion, for instance. So, say you were overcome by an impulse to view pornography. You would then pull out a whoopee cushion to help redirect the impulse, then push the button on the One-Impulse Time Machine watch. Of course, you must be careful about introducing this prompt into your environment, as this, in and of itself, could register as a new impulse."

"How would I be careful?"

"I would say the prompt, or the whoopee cushion in this case, must be introduced automatically without much conscious thought."

"Hmmm..."

"And the last point of note. The new prompt that you choose should be intrinsically valuable. I used the whoopee cushion as an example, because humor fits this profile, as humor is intrinsically valuable."

"I think I understand. But, to clarify, what if I pushed the button twice, three times, four times? Could I keep traveling back in time? Or does this have the same restriction as the other device? As I sit here thinking about it, I could solve a whole lot of my problems if I could push the button a couple hundred times."

Barrantine chuckled. "Good question. As with the One-Sentence Time Machine, it only works on one impulse at a time. Pushing it twice does nothing. It's a limitation of the technology. So, would you like to give this a try?"

46 – Martin's Experiments with Impulses

Martin looped the One-Impulse Time Machine watch around his wrist. On a coffee table to his right, a vaporizer burned red, along with a bag of weed, a beer, his computer and a bowl of wasabi almonds. Placing a purple lace strand of OG Kush in the vaporizer, he inhaled and chased it with a gulp of Titan IPA. Martin's brain started to relax. He hit play on Father John Misty's *I Love You, Honeybear.* Bad idea. He and Ana both loved this CD and had listened to it dozens of times together. Over the years, the album had evolved into a symbol of strength and humor in their relationship, of the bond holding them together through thick and thin. Martin hit stop only a minute into the first song.

What should he play instead? An upbeat album to take his mind off Ana and his unemployed status? Pokey Lafarge's *Something in the Water* sounded pretty-good. He extracted the CD from its case. Wait a minute, was it time to give the One-Impulse Time Machine a go?

Martin pushed the button.

Shebang.

The impulse to listen to Pokey morphed into Shabazz Palaces.

Folk to experimental rap music.

Martin put Shabazz Palaces in, leaned over the coffee table, took another pull on the vaporizer and lit a candle. The album worked. Thoughts of Ana drifted away, at least for the time being. He stood up, started to dance. Spinning, bouncing on the balls of his feet, he skated across the square brown rug in front of the speakers. Three songs later, a different mood rushed forward, the grand patriarch of moods himself—Mr. Boredom.

Or was it boredom? Maybe it was conjured boredom, a hidden desire to test Barrantine's invention to the fullest extent, to gauge his own level of progress in the counseling? Or perhaps it was another species of boredom? Like weary boredom. Or reflective boredom. Or boredom supreme. Or Sartrean boredom, digging in its heels, aware of itself, aware that there is no exit, no escape.

Naturally, the desire for pornography entered his mind.

Martin pushed the button on the One-Impulse Time Machine watch.

Bam, his cognitions turned turtle.

Thoughts of porn went up in smoke. Now images of Seattle rushed in. Flying off curbs on his skateboard at 3:00 AM. Past homeless people covered in newspaper. Past tinted windows. Past blurry reflections. Past hookers with heels so tall they could barely walk.

Martin opened the fridge. Why not give the device another test run? A Mercenary IPA sounded good. He pushed the button. Canasta! The desire to have a Mercenary IPA was washed down the drain like a bomber of spoiled beer. Now he now wanted an entirely different drink, a gin and tonic. So, the device worked again, and apparently Barrantine was right. His randomly changing impulses did indeed seem to be the product of a bunch of half-crocked electrons hopping around in his brain. But did the One-Impulse Time Machine work sufficiently? Could it survive the test of viewing actual porn? Martin felt obligated to find out.

He fired up his computer and entered several illicit websites at once: sluttywives.com, makemykittypurr.net, japenesenympho.tv, serviceyourneeds.org, milfsnmilk.xxx. Each of the websites was arousing in its own way. The silicone breasts. Soft, shiny asses. Pop-ups of famous stars and their secret tapes. Kim Kardashian. Serena Williams. Amber Rose. Martin popped the top button off his pants. The impulse was robust, fertile, fully nurtured.

He pushed the button.

The desire to bend Amber Rose over backwards was gone.

But Amber's lips were full. Her breasts were round. Her ass and shaved vagina were worth savoring for their own sake, a cornucopia of soft and supple treasures for the senses. So the desire came back. But what about Barrantine's suggested method of having a prompt to divert his impulses? Martin walked into the kitchen, pulled a photograph of Ana off the fridge. Back to the computer. Back to Amber Rose. Back to the Storm. The rain. The lighting. The deafening pound of thunder. Hail. Rotation. A funnel cloud.

Martin examined the picture of Ana.

He pushed the button on the One-Impulse Time Machine.

The thunder stopped. The rain dissipated. Blue skies emerged. The Storm cleared. Martin clicked out of the porn site, sunk into the couch and reflected on his successful experiment with impulses. Feels good, he thought. Progress was made. The fending off of a Temptress. But what would happen when the urges arose spontaneously, in an uncontrolled environment, under the pressure of geothermal features, or cracks in the lithosphere, where water and fire meet, where subduction and seduction become one?

47 – Diver Neurons Are Lost

"That shit was whack," said Zeke, referring to Banshee's torn jeans, her cottage cheese ass, funky wail, eyes sunken-in like a crack whore, dirty ass makeup, saggy tits and deception about her English language skills. "Let's put that fishy bitch in the rearview mirror fast as possible."

Everyone agreed. Wise leadership, they thought. Perhaps Zeke had garnered a few things from Chuck. Yet, even though they were now 500 fathoms deep and two miles away from Banshee, the same set of problems persisted. The water was warm and off-color. There were no mermaids to be found. Their eardrums hurt from the loud wail. The tips of their penises still burned as if poked with a branding iron.

"I wonder if we should swim closer to the surface," said Desmond. "We might have better luck finding mermaids."

Zeke's lower jaw stuck out while he pondered. "Aight man, I'm game. You wanna lead the way?"

Surprised by the offer, Desmond adjusted his head lamp. "Sounds good. Should we head east?"

"Your call."

With a firm swish of his dendrites, Desmond set off into the ocean blue.

An hour passed.

"Can you smell that?" asked Desmond.

"You talking 'bout cooch?" queried Zeke.

"Yeah, could be. Let's keep going."

Sure as shit, a quarter-hour later, a pungent conglomeration of pheromone molecules swaddled their noses. Although it was hard to tell what it signified—pussy, ass, etc.—the scent clearly made an impression.

"Hell, yeah," said Zeke, libido flaring up. "You notice anything different?"

"You mean the redness?" asked Desmond, noticing an auburn tint in the water.

"Uh-huh."

"I do see it, and it's odd. Red pheromones. Could be menstruation?"

"You talking 'bout the period?" asked Zeke.

"Yes," said Desmond.

"Ain't got no problems with that. You?"

"I guess not," said Desmond, prospecting the seafloor. "Hey, looks like we are hitting a seamount, or the base of one anyway."

"A what?" asked Zeke.

"Check it out. Those are mountains. We are climbing. Or, you know, not climbing, but following an uplift. I think those are lava columns and spires in the distance. Is that a hydrothermal vent?"

An hour later, they found themselves in front of a rock face.

"Final ascent," said Desmond, weaving over cracks and shadowy overhangs. "Let's be careful."

When they reached the top, they peered over the other side. To their surprise, the seamount leveled off, giving way to an expansive underwater plateau that went on for miles. They sat down on a ledge and scanned the seascape, hoping to find the source of the pheromones.

Zeke patted Desmond on the shoulder. "Is that what I think it is?"

"You mean the big ol' blue object moving between two rocks?"

"Yep."

"Looks like a damn sperm whale."

"The same one as before, actually. See the scars on its tail?"

Sensing it was being watched, the great beast turned in their direction. When it did, claw marks became visible on its head. Blood pooled around its mouth.

"Damn, what happened?" asked Zeke.

"I have no idea. Looks like it was attacked."

"I guess all the blood ain't from the period then."

"Right," said Desmond.

After a bit of banter about the gender of the sperm whale and the menstruation question (little did Desmond and Zeke know that sperm whales don't menstruate), the Diver Neurons decided to swim closer to try and get a better view. But as they did, the sperm whale rolled to its side and swam the opposite way.

Unsure which direction to go, Desmond and Zeke contemplated their next steps. Should they follow the sperm whale or not? What was the risk? What was the reward? Time was ticking away, and the answers were far from obvious.

"Maybe the sperm whale's injuries can tell us more about our own predicament," said Desmond, feeling oddly philosophical. "It seems like it's hurting just like we are."

"Yeah," said Zeke, noting a similar feeling in himself. "She definitely in pain."

48 – Ana Visits the Cafeteria

Ana sat down at her desk at Front Range Community College and scanned her email. With the summer semester in full swing, student complaints trickled in. The teachers were unfair and biased. Students were unaware that they had to cite sources. It was just a coincidence that the Turnitin plagiarism software reported a 75% similarity reading. Why are there so many writing assignments in the course? I'm an engineer, not an English major!

Normally Ana would dutifully mow through these issues, but her recent panic attacks made her gun-shy about the smallest challenges. Being in the grips of second-order anxiety, anything could trigger agoraphobia at a moment's notice, rendering her immobile, unable to do her job. Meetings felt intimidating. The basement hallways were dark, underground. The drive to work was congested, full of tailgaters, trucks with big exhaust pipes capable of squashing her Toyota Prius in the flick of a blinker. People, places, things. Ana's comfort level was shrinking, her reliance on Xanax expanding.

Time to mix it up.

Time to visit the bison on the open range, watch it feed on the grass.

Ana stood in the cafeteria line, surveyed the menu. Baked potatoes, pizza, tacos. Normally Martin's menus were less pedestrian, more interesting, and Ana pictured herself saying this when she saw him. All it would take is an icebreaker sentence, a word or two they could connect to, chuckle at, find common ground with. From here, Martin could take the lead with his humor, irony or courtliness, depending on his mood. And then, who knows, maybe a hug would follow. Oh, to be touched by Martin. Ana's shoulder blades tingled. Tension escaped her chest. The door to her own insecurities flew wide open.

But Martin was nowhere to be seen, and the bison in the grass started snorting, knocking up dust, lifting its hindquarters as if it were ready to buck. Ana had committed herself to the thought of seeing Martin, yet the thought had no referent. Reality was, therefore, unstable, unreliable, full of third level modal anxiety—the fear of fearing the possibility of being in fear. Ana wanted to talk, needed to talk; her self-preservation instinct screamed out "I miss you!" No more principles. No more rational analysis. No more ego. No more pride. Ana sympathized with Martin's infidelity. His actions were understandable, she thought. No one is innocent. There's always a reason.

"Hi, Mrs. Ana," said the cashier. "That'll be $4.95."

Ana handed the cashier a five. "Where's Martin today?" She couldn't resist.

"Didn't you know?" said the cashier. "Martin quit."

Quit?

Ana felt faint as she placed change from the cashier into her purse. Humiliation followed.

"I had no idea."

Ana made the dark trek back to her office via the basement route. She sat down. Questions bounced off the walls of the room making divots in the dry wall. Should she call Martin? Text him? Had he met another woman? Or perhaps she should end the relationship now? Send him divorce papers? Was she ready for that? Ana reached into her purse, popped a Xanax in acknowledgment of the unilateral nature of her own vulnerability.

Where the *hurter* is free, forgives himself, is absolved.

And the *hurtee* continues to hurt, feels new levels of pain when there should be a sense of freedom from doing no wrong.

The *hurter* explains why he did the hurting. "I'm a product of circumstance who was put in a situation causing me to act unlike myself."

The *hurtee* just feels the pain, struck by her own sensitivity and weakness, her Achilles heel tender to the touch. "I'm weak, I'm tired, I'm sad. Please forgive me for not being stronger, more available."

The *hurter* hurts less when he should hurt more.

The *hurtee* hurts more when she should hurt less.

No justice in the pain, Ana picked up the phone and started to dial Martin's number. She stopped herself, took a bite of taco. The meat was dry and tasted like dirt. She spit it out. Her appetite disappeared. She picked up the phone again and dialed the full number. The phone rang through, all the way through to the end, ringing and ringing and ringing into oblivion. Evidently, Martin had disabled his messaging system.

Ana's heart beat fast. Her fingers tingled. Dusty images hovered around her periphery. Images from the months before her father died. The opacity, the gloom, the heaviness, as he lumbered through the house at half speed, half alive, feet submerged in a mud, unkempt, pretending very poorly he would find a new job soon. Ana didn't want to reveal her concerns to her father, felt she needed to pretend he was doing fine. Ana took her cues from her mother, from the trance-like state she was in, makeup applied three layers thick, wood floors so clean they shined like a lantern.

Ana set down her phone and closed a drawer on her desk. Knees weak, she stumbled into her boss' office.

"I'm not feeling good. I feel nauseous. I think it's the flu. If it's all right with you, I'm going to take sick leave and work from home."

49 – A Change of Direction

Turns out Martin did not quit his job, but was asked to leave. He'd been mailing it in for months now. Even before the flooding, his attention to detail was scattered, sloppy, "blasted from an old blunderbuss" were the words his boss used. Scheduling errors. Forgetting to purchase basic supplies like napkins and olive oil. Coming to work late. Martin's mind had been displaced by bad decisions and marital woes that compounded, spilling over into his work life. When things are off in one area, they tend to be off in others.

But this was not a first. Martin knew joblessness. He knew it from the seasonal and not so seasonal jobs he worked in his early twenties when he was a cook for a children's camp off Orcas Island, or a pantry chef in Yellowstone Park's Roosevelt Lodge. Later, when he was twenty-eight years old, he and a friend quit their jobs, decided to drive across the country to Daytona Beach for a two-month spring break to party during the night and cook or bartend during the day. But shortly after they arrived, Martin went night surfing and broke his ankle. Food stamps and the good graces of his friend were the only buoys keeping him afloat during those months of recovery.

Martin perused his resume, which sat on the kitchen table. Sous chef. Kitchen manager. Bar back. Fry cook. Server. Dishwasher. He'd done it all. Martin pressed his face to the screen door to get a blast of fresh air, then pulled away, panned to the One-Impulse Time Machine watch, which clung to his wrist like a starfish on a pier. "What the fuck?" he said, pushing the button on the watch just to see if it had dual functionality and could retract sentences. But nothing seemed to change. As far as Martin could tell, the words still held true, as did all the other shit in his life. No wife, no job, his condo needed repairs, he was seeing a counselor, he drank too much, he was abusing a wrist watch on this arm and flouting time travel itself.

So what next? Which direction to turn? Where to find purpose, meaning, stability, in the face of wavering emotions and fundamental change? Last week saw progress. This week feels bleak. Like a bumblebee in search of nectar, Martin's general outlook could change in the blink of an eye. Yesterday, the bumblebee finds a flower. It feels nourished, energized, alive. Today, splat. The bumblebee meets its fate on a windshield.

The owner of the car engages the wipers.

Martin turns into a yellow smear.

Where was all this leading?

The skin on Martin's face pulled tight. Never before had he felt so far away from *Meaning*, so close to the *Windshield*, where all it would take is a second for the cold, heartless, unforgiving piece of glass to make its presence known, for Martin to feel the fragile nature of his own consciousness, how quickly self-awareness and optimism can transform into helplessness, doubt, fear and trembling.

Turning to his bookshelf, Martin lifted Chef Gordon Ramsay's *Passion for Flavor* from the bottom shelf. He began paging through the recipes and old note cards tucked into the pages, plunging into words, into food, searching for a new kind of spark. Ramsay really did cook with fire. The simplicity, the flair, fine ingredients and provocative pairings. Sea bass with fennel and lemon capers. Coconut pancakes with mango slices and lime syrup. Barrantine was right about chefs being drawn toward the visceral, the life sustaining, hands-on construction of organic matter, which they confronted daily, funneling their inner turbulence, their shadows, into consumable artistry, into a culinary voice from *Parts Unknown*.

Dad, where did you go?
Dad, why can't I come too?
Dad, let me come home.
Dad, I just want to be with you.

Martin plucked another book off the shelf from the second row. Rachael Ray's *30 Minute Meals*. A different read entirely, Ana gave him the book years ago. At the time, the gift felt prosaic, uninspired. Rachael Ray? Really? But at this moment, the book had transformed into a sage piece of advice, Ana's finger resting on Martin's culinary pulse, where delicious comfort food met precision. No muddling in the middle ground. Clear temporal distinctions, fresh ingredients, clean greens, tight execution, bursting flavors that sing in distinct identifiable notes. Rice often served as the foundation.

While the rice cooked, vegetables steamed, sauces simmered and meats seared. Entire meals were assembled in the thirty-minute time frame. Thirty was a nice number. Time was not slipping away. Every moment mattered. Every moment had meaning. The oven of Martin's youth was on broil. The edge of his shadow crusted over with burnt cheese.

Honk!

A horn blasted from out of nowhere. Martin closed the book, slid open his screen door and peeked his head outside. A shitty old bread truck screeched to a stop; exhaust poured from the muffler. A man got out and transferred trays of bread from one truck to another. For a second, Martin wanted to tell the man to get his truck fixed, that the smell of exhaust was nauseating and in violation of emission laws.

Martin pushed the button on the One-Impulse Time Machine. Interestingly, the impulse to yell went away, and a stream of interconnected thoughts shuffled in...Chef Ramsey, *30 Minute Meals*, Ana, his unemployed status, a new category of work, his desire for change, time itself, caring about time, his dad, his mom. Martin shut the sliding glass door. Wait a minute. Bread truck. Food truck. *My own food truck.*

Maybe this was the answer, the change of direction he needed, a break from stagnation, a reorientation toward Meaning, a true form of channeling. Getting back to his roots. Back to rediscovering what cooking truly meant to him. The creativity and freedom were certainly there. He could design his own menu, his own theme, on his own time and schedule. Most of the breweries in Denver employed food trucks. He could cook at his favorite places and participate in food-beer pairings. Each location would be different. Each item on his menu completely his own. He would never step in the same river twice, never dip his paddle in the same part of the sea a second time.

Martin crumpled up his resume, opened his computer and began to browse the net for what it would take to purchase a food truck, the licensing, the demand, etc. Did he have the financial wherewithal to make it happen? Yes, he did. Thanks to Ana, he was debt free, and his Credit Karma score registered 760. Martin studied the Denver skyline. Greyness. A slight rain came down. The skin on Martin's face relaxed. He felt lighter, excited, like an anchor had been cut away that kept him from traveling to different parts of himself.

To Pier 62 at the Pike Place Market, legs dangling off the dock, under the light of a full moon.

To tunnels.

To the smell of fresh king salmon and halibut cheeks.

To the hard bop cadence of cars and trucks.

To the bedroom window he would sneak out of at night when it was time to explore.

50 – Nate's New Mystery

Over towering sea swells and glistening pools of white foam, Nate paddled hard to keep up with the sperm whale. As if a celestial galaxy had formed on the surface of the Sea, a cosmic splash art of the soul, Nate followed the wake of the great beast and the eruptions from its spout. Like an astronomer surveying the night sky, he sought patterns, connections and elusive spaces in the oceanic ether to guide his direction of travel. Frightening as it was to follow the elegant beast, the Sea was not like he'd been taught as a child. Evil was nowhere to be found. Beauty was everywhere. Connectedness. A sense that the wind, waves, whiteness and whale were part of one galactic mural.

Hours passed, miles followed. Only the moon illuminated the path of the sperm whale as it moved through the night in long sweeping turns and plunges into the heart of the Sea. Occasionally the whale would disappear for minutes, and Nate worried that it was gone. But just when it appeared all hope was lost, the whale would resurface and slow down, as if it were aware of Nate's presence.

Daybreak came at 5:30 AM. Splashes of water from the blowhole of the sperm whale pattered Nate's brow. Nate examined the splashes. Red, slightly viscous, blood came to mind, and Nate's stomach dropped at the thought of what it meant. But best not to rush to judgment, get too carried away with the possibilities. Even if the water was tinged with blood, perhaps this was a natural cycle of the sperm whale. "Focus on the positive," Nate repeated to himself. Remember what truly matters. His love of adventure, quest to discover the truth. His passion for mystery. His father. If only Pastor Samuel could see his son right now. Surely, he would be proud of Nate's persistence, his commitment to doing what he loved.

Nate paddled on and on and on through the piercing sun, through wind that cracked his lips, over rogue waves and unpredictable currents threatening to send him off course. Four in the afternoon. The ocean changed character; its current strengthened, became more focused. Longer, thicker waves propelled him forward. The color of the water darkened. Viridian blue intermingled with crimson red. Nate wiped salt from his eyes, tried to find the sperm whale in the textured seas. But the beast swam away, nowhere to be found. Only bubbles and a pool of auburn foam remained.

Nate's eyes circled the horizon. They circled again. On the third pass, he noticed an object in the distance, a mound of sorts sitting in the middle of the ocean half a mile away. The object didn't swim, didn't move, and Nate imagined it had legs attached to the sea floor. The hackles on back of his neck spiked. His vision seesawed. On an empty stomach, Nate worried he was hallucinating, tricked by the foibles of the Sea.

With no time to think, he centered himself in the life raft and tried to balance it the best he could, as it picked up speed. The water grew shallow. Waves broke around him. The water became crystal-clear as a colossal swell carried him over a coral reef. Looking down, Nate noticed eels slithering in and out of limestone shards, and reef sharks lurking beneath the surface. A school of jellyfish. Loggerhead turtles. Seahorses that luminesced in the shadows of the gangly limestone. Nate flew over a prism of metallic colors straight toward the mammoth object waiting in the distance.

Wham!

His boat came to a grinding halt when it struck the sand. He got out, stood in knee-deep water and watched the world wobble from side to side. A grove of palm trees, twisted and snarled driftwood, cliffs so high they touched the clouds.

Full of trepidation and wonder, he began walking along the beach. Passing by stone crabs, sand dollars and strange impressions in the sand, some resembling footprints, Nate wondered how a land within the Sea could happen. Not a single Angel Neuron had ever mentioned the possibility of an island, nor was it written about in scripture. In fact, the Angel Neurons didn't even have a proper word for such an occurrence, and as far as Nate could tell, their minds were devoid of the very idea. Perhaps the notion of an island would crumble their worldview or undermine the Sea-as-Hell myth. On the other hand, maybe the island was unsafe. Only time would tell. Yet, at that moment, Nate felt a certain confirmation about his journey, a sense of arriving at a place of great consequence, that even though danger could be lurking in the jungle, the island felt restorative, imbued with mystery.

51 – Ana's Father

Ana's legs were crossed, back slumped. Head hanging low, she had difficulty making eye contact with Barrantine, who examined his notes and wondered if he should tell Ana about his recent sessions with Martin. Certainly, this is what a normal counselor would do. He would find it prudent, even ethically necessary, to be up-front. But Barrantine was never one for blindly accepting conventional wisdom. To the contrary, the dynamic that was unfolding among all three parties encouraged him—the mystery, the tension, the acknowledgement of the healing potentiality of opposing forces.

"Ana, how have you been doing?" he asked softly.

Mazzy walked over, rubbed on Ana's leg.

"Not so good," she said, her voice weak. "I've been having the panic attacks again."

Barrantine's lower jaw protruded forward, as if he could feel her pain. "I'm sorry to hear this. Tell me what's been going on."

"Well, to be honest, I was starting to feel slightly better, and the fog began to lift. So I decided to stop by and see Martin in the cafeteria at work."

"And how did that go?"

"He wasn't there. The cashier told me he quit his job."

Barrantine feigned ignorance. "Quit? I wonder why?"

"No idea. But my anxiety kicked in heavy."

"I'm sure you were taken aback. Out of curiosity, what did you intend to say to Martin?"

"I'm not sure. I had a lot of mixed feelings. A part of me wanted to confront him, tell him what a jerk he was. Remind him about what I've done for him. Tell him to take ownership of his baggage. Let him know he has real issues...besides the cheating." Ana bit her lower lip. "The other part of me wanted to give him a hug because I miss him."

"Ana, you are being very honest here, both with yourself and me. And what happened after you realized Martin was not in the cafeteria?"

"I tried calling him, but he didn't answer. At that point, I started to feel myself spiral."

Barrantine leaned back in his chair. "Like when your father died?"

The question caught Ana off guard. "Kind of, I guess."

"Would you mind if I asked you a few questions about your father?"

"Sure."

"Before he died, what was going on with you and your family? What was the climate like in your household at the time? Was it similar to what you described before, where feelings were hidden?"

"To a degree, yes, but the bigger issue was my dad losing his job and gaining a lot of weight, and just not doing well. His whole face turned red; he had a dark aura. And since my dad was always home job hunting my parents' routine changed. They weren't used to spending that much time together. I think that's when it all started to add up. I'm sure losing his job was difficult, especially for someone from his generation. He was a proud man. With the expectation to be the provider, I know it had to hurt."

"Makes sense. I'm sure he did feel a real weight. And, if you don't mind me asking, in what manner did he take his life? How did you discover it?"

"My dad died in the mountains, in a meadow, actually, outside of Steamboat. He ended his life with a shotgun. I had no idea my dad still owned a gun. He used to bird hunt years ago, but I thought he had sold his guns. Anyway, my mom and I were out of town at the time visiting my grandmother. We found the note when we came home. He told us that he loved us but couldn't go on any more. He apologized over and over in the letter."

The sun was setting. A flock of sparrows flew by. Barrantine lowered the shades. "That must have been so difficult, the sadness overwhelming. Were there any other notable emotions you were experiencing at the time, any frustration or anger, for example?"

Ana breathed in slowly, ran her fingers through her hair. "No, I didn't blame him. He loved me and my mom dearly. He just couldn't see his way out of the darkness."

"And in the years after, when you were with Martin, did you discuss this with him specifically? Did you discuss the suicide directly?"

"A little bit. Funny enough, Martin was taking a philosophy class at one point, and we discussed *The Myth of Sisyphus*, which actually made me feel better. I know suicide was not supported in the book, but to me, the author made it more understandable in a way. Neither Martin nor I are religious, so I could relate. Are you familiar with the book?"

Barrantine rubbed his hands together. "Oh, yes...a classic. And I, too, appreciate Camus' intellectual treatment of suicide in the book, in terms of finding meaning in a world that might be godless in a traditional sense."

"Martin still mentions it. I think the book made a real impression."

"Anything else? Any other important moments come to mind...between you and Martin I mean?"

"Not really. I just appreciated him being there for me."

"Indeed. But I'm curious, do you feel like there are facets of your father's passing that went unprocessed?"

Ana sighed. "Probably."

"Any particulars come to mind?"

"I just think it left a dark cloud over my life in ways. When you experience this type of loss with a parent, you worry that you are destined for a similar fate. Maybe I started to overcompensate."

Barrantine recalled Martin making similar comments about his own father. "Fair enough. I can only imagine one would take certain mental steps toward adapting to the trauma and protecting one's self, if you will. Tell me how you might have overcompensated."

Ana thought carefully. "It probably made me more intense around work and finances."

"I see. So perhaps there was a fear around job security based on your father's experiences with losing his job?"

"Possibly."

"Any other areas of your life affected by your loss, any domains where a sense of security or control felt paramount?"

Ana's chin dipped down as she considered one of the driving factors that led her and Martin into counseling. "Maybe intimacy," she said. "Martin always told me that I don't know how to relax, that I am inhibited in ways. He said our relationship would be better, I would be happier, if I learned how to relax. And he could be right. Maybe I am uninspired when it comes to intimacy. Maybe I made it easier for him to cheat."

"No, no, Ana. I don't believe that is the appropriate conclusion here at all. Although everyone has room to grow, let's be clear. Martin betrayed you. He betrayed his original role of being there for you, of being a partner who helped you work through your father's death. Martin was disloyal to you as a friend, as a husband." Barrantine placed a colored pencil behind his ear. "I also gather that Martin's issues, if you will, with respect to emotional intimacy and the like, might stem from his own overcompensation structures—from his relationship with his mother, certainly, and perhaps with his father too."

"You should hear the stories," said Ana.

"Right, so let's be honest with ourselves here. However much you might desire to move past certain emotional barriers, Martin needs to follow your lead, but in a more significant way. Moreover, Martin's challenges are moral in nature. Yours are not. And with that, one can only hope his change in job status is grounded in moral reparation, in wholeness."

52 – Food Truck

Since Martin decided to start a food truck, life was changing by the day. After signing off on a loan to purchase an 18-foot 2014 Ford Gasoline, two breweries had already agreed to try out his new food truck concept—street tacos with international flair. Each of the seven continents would be represented. Tortillas made fresh daily. Fresh vegetables and meats seared over high heat on a flat top griddle. Gone were the days of prepping mac and cheese for 300 students. No more scrubbing burned pans until his fingers were raw. No more commute. No more dragging his ass out of bed at 7:00 AM. No more Sea. No more Storm.

Going forward, Martin would be his own boss and cook the food he wanted. Clean. Quick. Hot. Timely. Ready to order. The One-Impulse Time Machine watch on his wrist. A picture of Ana in her bathing suit taped to the interior of the food truck. Although Ana hated the picture, the move made therapeutic sense. Each time Martin was distracted by a summer dress, or an extra tight pair of booty shorts, he could push the button, rubberneck to the photo, and the illicit impulses would disappear into the crispy pork carnitas sizzling on the griddle.

The blackened catfish tacos layered with hominy salsa and old bay slaw. Green coconut curry sauce. Pineapple. Raw onions. Cilantro.

No uncouth impulse would go unchecked. No amount of yearning to see what was underneath those cutoff jeans would take Martin away from the task at hand. Only the food would matter, only his life ambitions, his attempt to understand and correct what had gone wrong with his marriage, with himself.

But, as it happened, on his first night at Odyssey Beerwerks, the evening did not go according to plan. Although the customers were satisfied, and the flavors were good, the food truck barely pulled in $100 in four hours. On top of that, Martin forgot to purchase a couple key ingredients and could only offer tacos from five continents. Although Martin's focus was clear, his mind connected to what he valued intrinsically, what was healthy for him, the result was less than he had hoped. Sure, he made it through the evening without the One-Impulse Time Machine, but did this matter, if he couldn't survive on a food truck salary?

Martin stood at the bar, ordered an Imperial Red Ale and chatted with the owner of the brewery. "Everyone seemed to really like the food," said the owner. "The diversity of flavors, the Thai and lamb tacos were especially great. I'm sorry there weren't more customers. But I suppose that's just how it goes, right?"

Just how it goes?

Martin's psyche felt tender to the touch. His emotions swerved like a car trying to miss a deer at sundown. Tire marks. Screeching. What if the food truck was a total failure? What if every night was *just how it goes?* What would Ana think? How would she respond? Although it was way too early to rush to judgement, Martin suspected her feelings would be mixed, her sense of uncertainty heightened. She could easily walk away for good, if she hadn't already.

Turning on his phone, he stared at an old photo of Ana standing on a ledge overlooking Heart Lake. What an awesome day. Effortless conversation. Perfect weather. A five-course lunch. Solitude. Wine. Love making. But what was real? Was Heart Lake real, or the breaking of Ana's heart? Martin's fingers tingled. The urge to call Ana was strong.

But what would he say?

That he loved her, missed her, was sorry he had been such a jerk? That even though he wasn't making a lot of money, his life was moving in a good direction with the counseling and the food truck? That he was trying to be the best person he could be?

But was his best really good enough?

If history was a guide, the answer was no. Martin had never walked the straight and narrow for an extended period of time, never truly stuck to his values when it came to women. His intentions were fine, his desire for moral correctness commendable. But his execution failed, his ability to say no when it counted was weak—no to the temptations, the horniness, the desire to shelve his own past, the sleet and hail, the moon and the tides, the undertow, the jagged rocks under the Sea.

So what now?

Even if Ana wanted to talk and was willing to reunite, would it really make sense in light of Martin's history and his current financial uncertainty? When the thunder roared and the lighting flashed, could he take stock of the situation, be a true weatherman, anticipate and prepare for strong winds, rotation? And if he couldn't, or wouldn't, or didn't fully want to, what would it mean?

What would it *really* mean
when the sinner continues to sin
feels weak, imbalanced, misunderstood
wants to scream out, that it was not all his fault
that he was not given a fair shot
that the quills on a pufferfish have purpose,
not all bad,
that crop circles for mating rituals are complicated
not meant for just anyone?

Martin put his phone in his pocket and scanned the brewery. Old bags of malts. Shiny fermenting tanks with horizontal reflections stood tall like watch dogs guarding a vault. A string of lights flickered in and out. A cedar gazebo. Slotted shadows over the pouring station, where names "Ghost Drifter Pale Ale" and "Psycho Penguin Vanilla Porter" were written on a chalkboard. The whole scene made Martin reflect on his upbringing. His mom. His dad. Two large silhouettes with no center, backs facing the sun.

Dad, you a crooked tree hanging over a ledge.
Mom, you a boulder about to roll.
Dad, how come didn't you save me?
Mom, you should know.

Martin swallowed his last drink of beer, set a twenty on the counter and stepped into the cool, damp air outside Odyssey Beerwerks. Glasses misted over, he wiped his lenses with his sleeve and contemplated the night sky. The moon shone bright. Teeth white craters were visible at her center. Jagged stars. A layer of auburn haze.

A halo.

53 – The Meaning of Life

Martin walked over to the window behind Barrantine's desk and pointed down to the street.

"Check it out," he said.

Barrantine swiveled around in his leather chair to see the colorfully decorated food truck Martin had named World Tacos. He smiled. "Yours?"

"Yep, bought it right after we talked."

"That quickly?"

Martin's head dipped down. "Possibly a little too quick. The truck didn't make a lot of money on its first couple days out."

"I see. Well, it's early. It takes time to establish a new business."

"True."

"What led to this exciting new idea?"

Martin lifted his arm in the air. "The watch, for one. I was using the One-Impulse Time Machine the other night, trying to do some channeling and whatnot. I guess you can say, I succeeded."

"Yes, but I'm hearing apprehension in your voice. Perhaps you can describe the nature of your channeling a bit more? What were you doing? What were you trying to channel from?"

"Hard to say. It all happened pretty quickly. I guess when I lost my job, I felt a certain heaviness, and I started asking all kinds of questions. I'm talking really basic questions. Like who I really am as a person, and what is meaningful to me, truly meaningful, if anything at all?"

"Sounds like an existential moment."

"I guess so. Do you ever experience that?"

"A loss of meaning? Sure, of course. I think we probably all do in our own ways. One day the world feels imbued with meaning. Scoring a free ticket to a concert. Running into a person who you haven't seen for a long time. The next day, nothing. Or, worse than nothing, as the world feels quite hollow with emptiness being the dominant theme."

"And which do you think is right?"

"Do you mean which perspective on meaning do I think is right?"

"Yes."

"Oh, I suppose when I sum it up, I lean toward there being something greater. I'm not talking religion here, but greater in terms of a transcendent spirit or consciousness." Barrantine cocked his head to the side. "Perhaps like neurons are to the brain. What I mean is that no single neuron is aware of how it functions in the greater consciousness of an organism. No single neuron is aware of its role in consciousness. But each neuron has a function. Each neuron is a part of a greater whole. We could be like that. Our lives could be much the same."

"Hmmm..."

"And what about you, Martin? Do you believe in any form of transcendence? Have you traditionally been religious or spiritual?"

"Not really. Growing up, my mom used to take me to church, but I'm pretty sure she just felt obligated. Personally, I couldn't relate. Asking Jesus into my heart, praying, all of it seemed like a bunch of nonsense." Martin shrugged his shoulders. "Then you throw in the ugly stories about pastors molesting little kids."

"Understood. Conventional religion is not for everyone, and personally, I can very much appreciate rejecting it. Yet, in terms of the meaning question, it is fair to ask, if not religion, then what? Now, I personally believe we have an answer to this question, but it is tricky nonetheless."

"And what is your answer?" asked Martin.

Barrantine leaned forward. "My answer...engagement with the little things in life...and the big things. I'm talking deep, active engagement with what is before us, with what we are good at, with what we have a calling for, such as being a chef. It is my belief that people who create, artists in particular, are closer to the source of meaning. With that said, I'd like to ask you more about your channeling. In the midst of your job hunting, what led to the food truck idea in particular? What were you considering at the time?"

"Ummm...I was exploring cookbooks and whatnot, trying to find a different head space. And, yeah, I was polishing up my resume. Then I started tinkering with the watch." Martin pulled a frayed photograph from his wallet. "Prior to that, I was admiring a picture of Ana."

"Ah, so you used Ana for your prompt?"

"Right, per your advice, I was trying to tap into what mattered to me personally."

"Makes perfect sense. Then what?"

"Then, I started pondering the stuff we talked about, like how I used cooking as escape from my upbringing and how I was bored with the cafeteria job. Eventually, one thought led to another, and I was struck with the idea to get a food truck. It all seemed very random, but it made perfect sense at the time. I even imagined Ana would love the idea."

"And are you now suggesting Ana would not love the idea?"

"Kind of. I mean, the food truck didn't make a lot of money on its first two nights."

"Aren't you are being a little hard on yourself?"

Martin put his hands behind his head and looked at titles on Barrantine's bookshelf. *Entropy. Fight Club. Lila. Under the Skin.* On the far end of the bookshelf, William Hjortsberg's

Falling Angel stuck out slightly. Interesting title, he thought to himself. Dark, strange, paradoxical.

Falling

Angel

"I guess it funneled into several questions I have," said Martin.

"Such as?"

"Such as whether or not I can really change, and what that change would involve. Could I pay the bills? Would I be the person Ana married? Would this be too outside the box for her?"

Barrantine pulled the shades down. "I understand what you are saying, yet maybe Ana wants to step outside the box, perhaps she even needs to in her own way. Remember that lifestyle changes can be just what the doctor ordered, in that they can give people a new framework, an increased awareness of what each person needs, wants, is capable of. And it's early. You just started the business. Let it steep. Let it simmer. In the meantime, I applaud your decision. And not only do I applaud it, but I would encourage you need to continue to step outside the box, to explore new opportunities, to not fear taking risks."

Barrantine adjusted his seat. "Remember the scene in *The Matrix* when Neo was given the choice to take the red pill or blue pill?"

Martin nodded. "Of course. That's a classic scene."

"Well, I think that when you decided to come back into counseling, you essentially swallowed the red pill, which is the pill of truth about the real world—the real world within. Now I think you need to continue to explore this world and let it guide you to new experiences."

54 – The Oracle

Near an estuary on the southern coast of Martin's occipital lobe, where fluctuating serotonin levels mingled with moonlit images of a hopeful future, Nate wiped sand out of his hair. Having slept on the beach for twelve hours straight, he stood up, stretched and inspected the bay. Expecting to see the same white water and chop as he had the last three days, Nate noticed the Sea had changed character. Waves churned in a circular motion. The water turned rusty-red with cartilage-grey flecks floating on the surface. A halo emanated from the middle of the bay. Loud screams ripped through the morning sky.

Nate fixed his gaze on the halo's center. The eye of a storm came to mind. But this eye was different. Neither calm nor still, violence inhabited her center. Snarling, brooding, a battle between two seagoing beasts was taking place. Attacker and victim. Predator and prey. One feasting on the underbelly of the other, blood pouring from the victim's orifices, pectoral fins and tail torn away, internal organs exposed. Howling at the moon, the attacker wore a black cape that popped like a snare drum when it breached. The victim was dense, blue, oblong, an enormous mammal who flapped in pain as the attacker sucked from its bladder and reproductive tract.

For four straight days, the savagery continued. The wicked witch of the ocean blue feasting on the poor sperm whale like she was robbing its soul. Maroon waves crashed onto the shore. Fiery pools of blood glistened under cloudy skies. Sickened, Nate watched the situation with equal parts horror and fear, as hard questions pounded him. What did it mean that his spirit animal, the sperm whale, was being murdered? Had he been led into a trap? Stay or go? His stomach empty, mind tattered, Nate was at an impasse, his faculties beaten down by the sight of Banshee feeding on the sperm whale.

I need to pull out of this funk. I need to make a new decision. But what?

Nate slapped himself on the cheeks, reached into his backpack. Tinfoil. A water bottle and duct tape. A *water catch. Yeah, sounds like a good idea.* Nate cut out the plastic support tubing from his backpack, ran it from the water bottle to a saucer fashioned out of the tinfoil. He filled the Nalgene bottle with salt water, hoping it would percolate. Sure enough, in minutes water began to drip into the tinfoil saucer. Nate took a sip. Salt-free. Delicious. His spirits began to lift.

Time to let the last four days wash over him, discharge his emotions, focus on the present moment, on what he could control. Nate turned away from the Sea and sat down on a log. *Deep breaths*, he said to himself. Ignore the screams, the howling, the dark song of ecstasy. Let it pass. Let it all pass. All of experience. Time. Space. Rationality. The illusion of the self. Let it go. Let it all go...

Clap, clap, clap.

Until he couldn't.

What was that sound? A monitor lizard? A tiger? Bear? A banshee who walks on shore? Bushes rustled. Branches broke. Whistling.

The sound grew closer.

Clomp, clomp, clomp.

Just as Nate was ready to stand up and walk away, something emerged from the trees.

A lanky biped, precisely, with cannons for arms. The man moved toward Nate with the focus and flow of a mako shark. Fear scrambled through Nate's veins. Spiritual perspectives came to mind. The feeling of being in the presence of an unnamable force of nature, a being who held more knowledge in his left pinky than Nate did in his entire cellular body. The man wore Neoprene boots and a jean vest, and chewed snus or sunflower seeds.

"Howdy," said the man, extending his hand.

Nate could smell whiskey on his breath. "Uh, howdy."

"Name's Jonk-Q Mosileeleelee. But Jonk-Q is fine."

Weird name, Nate thought, shaking his hand. "Great, I'm Nate."

Jonk-Q leaned over and clutched the parachute. "What's this?" he asked.

"I came from up there," said Nate, pointing to the sky. "From the clouds. The parachute helped me get down."

"Right, I get that, but I'm not really sure you need it," said Jonk-Q, who next turned to Nate's life raft and slapped it. "Same with this. Time to ditch the boat, shave off all the unnecessary entities—I'm talking Ockham's razor type stuff—and focus on the task at hand." Mosileeleelee's toe tapped on the pools of blood under his feet. "See that Siren feasting on that poor sperm whale?" he said, pointing to the sea.

Nate stroked his chin. "Uh...Siren?"

"Yes, a Siren." Jonk-Q paused. "Ever heard of the *Odyssey?*"

"No."

"Well, basically, she's a black-caped sea filly who lives in our genes."

"Our jeans?"

"No, our genes," said Jonk-Q, hearing the error in Nate's tone of voice. "And our jeans," he said chuckling. "So, you need to go tangle with her."

"Tangle?"

"Yes, and tango," said Jonk-Q, speaking quite literally.

Nate was intrigued but struggled to follow Jonk-Q

Mosileeleelee's conversational level switches.

"So, I know what you are wondering," said Jonk-Q, "because I usually do. You're wondering *how* you are going to tangle with that black-caped sea filly who is feasting on that poor sperm whale."

"Pretty much," said Nate.

"Well, that's for you to figure out."

"And how would I go about that?"

Jonk-Q split open a sunflower seed shell and blew it into the air. The shell caught an updraft and comingled with a flock of egrets passing by.

"Kid, you have a radical nature, and you come from a good father. You're here to make your dad proud. And you're here to carry out the burden of the explorer. You're here to help people, to help non-people, navigate their futures. You're Odysseus of the *Odyssey*."

Nate shrugged his shoulders. "And who are you then?"

"Depends on who you ask. I've been called an Oracle. I've been called a Seer and a Prophet. Hell, I've been called a lot of different things. A lot of 'em ain't real good. But, if you ask me, I'm just a dude who knows about black-caped sea fillies. So, let me leave you with a little advice."

Jonk-Q snapped his fingers and a puma stepped out of the shadows.

"Don't shy away from uncertainty. And damn sure don't lose your sense of humor."

The puma hopped up into Jonk-Q's arms and spooned his neck.

"Because black-caped sea fillies can sense that kind of weakness and don't do well with jokes. Know what I mean?"

Nate did not know what Jonk-Q Mosileeleelee meant, but as he tried to find the right question to ask, Jonk-Q curled the puma's tail around the front of his neck, tipped his fingers goodbye and disappeared into the jungle.

55 – The Problem of Control

July. Sky grey. Moisture localized. Drizzle. Water logged. Rain pelting down on the skylight. Barrantine scanned his notes from Ana's last session, where they examined forces that bulldozed her thoughts, burying them in hidden layers in the dirt. Anxiety. Control. The repression and overcompensation following her father's death.

Ana wore a black fleece with a turtleneck and a scarf.

"Can I turn up the heat?" asked Barrantine.

"I'm fine," said Ana, staring at her lap like it was an island. "Just not feeling great today."

"I understand. Shall we just get started then?"

"Sure."

"Last week we left off talking about your father's death and how this may have manifested in a need to manage or control certain aspects of your life—finances or your job, for example. We further discussed how this sense of control could extend to other areas."

Ana looked up at the skylight. Leaves, dirty brown streaks ran down the center.

"Like intimacy?"

"Yes, intimacy was one possibility," said Barrantine, gazing into his journal. "Noting that, I'd like to take a step back and approach these issues in a more visual way. So, if we think of a person as a house, we can note that some houses have windows that tend to be closed, whereas other houses have windows that tend to be more open. With the former, the inside of the house is obviously protected from the elements like wind and rain. With the latter, the inside of the house is more susceptible to the elements. Of course, there are benefits to both states of affairs, but when the windows are open, one is closer to Mother Nature, so to speak."

Ana adjusted her purse, searching for a way to respond. As she did, a memory bubbled up. A party at her house during the summer when her dad was on break. She was a young girl, around ten years old. Faculty members gathered in an air-conditioned sunroom. Ana wandered around serving mini quiche on a plate.

Her mother peeked her head into the sunroom. "Should we open the door?" she said, with a smile.

"*What?*

Her father's face grew red. They had already discussed this. He was sensitive to the heat; he wanted the house to stay cool, needed the house to stay cool. He turned sharply to open the sliding glass door. Wham! A collision with Ana. The plate of quiche went flying. She fell into a bookshelf.

Ana was ejected from the memory. "Am I the house whose windows are closed up?" she asked.

"No," said Barrantine. "I'm not necessarily saying that. But perhaps the metaphor is worth discussing. So, if you don't mind, let's go back to when your father died. In what ways did your general outlook change after his death?"

"I'm not sure exactly. I probably became numb, more closed off to the world."

"And at what point did Martin enter in?"

"He came in a few years later."

"I recall that you said Martin helped take your mind off your father, in terms of being more active with traveling, hiking and such. Perhaps he helped you open up?"

"Yes, but then I probably closed myself off again."

"To Martin?"

"Right, especially after I became aware of his pornography

habits. I feel like it made me run the opposite direction—away from him, basically."

Barrantine scribbled a few notes and paged through his journal like he was tearing into a sack lunch. "Ana, I sense we are at an important juncture here. Even setting aside the question of how Martin factors in, it seems to me that further exploration of what it means for you to open up, to get back to the person you want to be, is warranted."

"I agree, but at this point, I wouldn't have a clue where to start."

The heater in Barrantine's office kicked on. Rumbling. Burnt dust smell.

"Understood, yet the first point I'd like to make is to be patient and not pressure yourself. If the windows on your house have been closed for any amount of time, they may have been painted over and hard to open. Which is normal. With that said, I would encourage you to challenge your spirit."

Ana shrugged her shoulders. "I'm honestly not sure what that means."

Barrantine lifted a cup of blood orange tea to his lips. "I think it means engaging your passions. Maybe a fun activity you haven't done for a while, where some type of exertion is present."

Ana loosened her scarf. "Would dancing qualify?"

"Yes!" said Barrantine. "Dancing would be wonderful. I recall that you love to dance. This seems like a great place to start, the point being that you should allow the breezes to enter the house, let a little wildness take over. The other suggestion I have is to read a book in which this wildness might be present, perhaps *Infinite Jest* by David Foster Wallace. Have you heard of it?"

"I've heard the name."

"Well, here's what I'll say about this book. It is, I believe, a model of excess, of a windy spirit trying to be itself through writing. I have always speculated that reading it can help one tap into the impulses residing within the windy spirit. And I mean this in a way where story matters less than style. It is the impact of the extreme style of the author that gives the reader a sense for this excess."

Ana was happy to have concrete suggestions from Barrantine. "Thank you," she said softly. "I will check it out."

"I think you should, and hang in there, Ana. I understand this is an extremely difficult time, but I am confident that taking these steps will be worth your effort and, difficult as they might be, will help bring you closer to the place you want to be, to where your spirit can fly."

Part 5: The Place from which Change is Possible

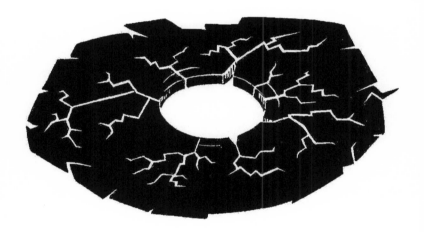

56 – Barrantine's Regret

Barrantine drove on I-70 to his vacation home outside of Winter Park. Normally he would try to clear his head with a few avant-garde jazz selections, but today he listened to audio recordings from recent counseling sessions. While the CD played, nagging concerns about his practice weighed heavy on his mind, as just last week a couple had refused further payment and demanded a refund. Before that, an explosive argument occurred leading to the dissolution of a relationship. More recently, Barrantine had been summoned to court, accused of "destabilizing his clients" and of "mocking time-tested counseling methods."

In his own mind, Barrantine could explain his apparent failures. Either couples were not prepared for the hard work marriage counseling takes, or they were not right for each other in the first place. On top of it all, the underlying quantum conditions of consciousness seemed to have a wildcard effect on any attempt to guide his clients toward normalcy.

But who was he kidding? A theme had developed over the years, and many of his own doubts had been confirmed. Instead of focusing on the importance of emotion in his practice, Barrantine was consumed with inventing. Instead of nurturing the interpersonal subjectivity of his clients, Barrantine wanted to talk metaphysics and epistemology. Instead of engaging with what really mattered, Barrantine had been playing it safe as a counselor, failing to evolve.

Turning up Berthoud Pass, he took a long pull off of an Australian Shiraz. Forwarding the CD to his most recent session, where he suggested that Ana "open up the windows on her house," he started to feel his worries diminish. "Solid advice," he mumbled to himself. "Practical, grounded, yet pushing toward growth." But just as a gust of wind hit the side of his Westphalia bus, the CD skipped to the place where he had recommended David Foster Wallace's *Infinite Jest*.

Barrantine pulled over on the top of Berthoud Pass and replayed his session with Ana. Shit. What was he thinking? He knew David Foster Wallace had committed suicide. Given what had happened with Ana's father, what kind of a counselor would recommend this book? Like the avant-garde jazz musicians he so adored—Coleman, Coltrane, Mingus, Monk, Davis—was Barrantine simply bouncing from one idea to the next, free-wheeling it, without concern for his clients? Distraught by his oversight, he downed the rest of his wine and began descending Berthoud Pass.

Now driving through Winter Park, he followed a gravel road that cut through a valley in the James Peak Wilderness. His mind moving from one anxious thought to the next, he drove for another hour, until he arrived at his cabin. When he stepped into the humble Douglas-fir structure, Barrantine was overcome with worry and began to weep. The countless nights laboring over his inventions. The grappling with fundamental paradoxes of the self. The painstaking questions aimed at solving the riddle of the human animal.

Reflecting on an old sketch of the One-Sentence Time Machine hanging on the wall, his emotions intensified even more. Barrantine had always been so proud of this particular invention. Not only did he believe it was revolutionary and might one day change our view of relationships, he also viewed it as a clever way to undermine our obsession with technology. But was something obscured by the cleverness? Had Barrantine really ever developed a strategy for weaning couples off of the time travel device? Although he may have led them to the place from which change is possible, had he ever helped couples walk the path once they got there—interpersonally, emotionally, phenomenologically, in radical subjective affirmation of the other?

A bottle of Colterris Cab from Palisade rested on the kitchen counter. Barrantine pulled the cork and placed the needle on Johnny Cash's *Orange Blossom Special*. Wincing in pain, tears streamed down his cheeks as Johnny and June sang, "When It's Springtime in Alaska." Although he never considered himself a true artist, he could relate to Cash's suffering. The pain of the search. The deficits and excesses of the creative impulse. Could he translate his empathy for Cash into a useful counseling methodology, one born of wisdom and the desire for transcendence?

Feverish and in need of fresh air, he meandered outside. The sun had dipped behind the mountains. Venus was a bright yellow speck on the horizon. With a pour of Colterris in one hand and a notebook in another, he followed a trail on his property, often stopping when the lighting was right to scribble down ideas or draw pictures with his colored pencils. At one point, he sketched out an elaborate rock wall that held faces suggesting the passage of time. Later, he drew a single tree hanging over a cliff. Barrantine walked to the edge of the rock face and screamed out:

"I'm here! What do you want from me?!"

Now walking along the rim of a canyon for a half-mile or so, until the trail gave way to a meadow with a small lake at the outskirts of his property, Barrantine sat beside the water's edge. As he did, his enormous Samsung cell phone jabbed into his side. Irritated, he reached into his pocket and extracted it. Barrantine applied pressure to the screen with his thumbs until the phone began to crack. Holding it close to his face one last time, he cocked his arm and launched it into the middle of the lake. The phone made a small splash and sunk to the weeds.

Barrantine stood up, hiked back to the cabin and began doodling in his journal. Swirling vortexes of color, Kandinsky-like sketches of stars, musical notes, an eye in the middle of the sky. He cracked open his closet. Four cans of paint. A brush. He unrolled a twelve-foot piece of canvas, laid it the driveway. Barrantine launched into a Jackson Pollock-inspired piece. Long waves of black and orange streaks coated the edges. Trails of green spiraled at its core. Paint dripped from his brush, from his hands, from his chin. Taffy. Cotton candy. A molten lava of textures. Barrantine's elbows were doused in blue, in yellow. He leaned over.

Dot. Dot. Dot. Dot. Dot.

Machine gun impressions along the top of the painting.

Whistling noises from his mouth. Howling, chortling, he dipped his hair into a can of orange paint. Not enough. Barrantine poured some over his head, rubbing the viscous acrylic goop into his hair like it was beard oil. He laid down and rolled across the top of the painting. Clouds formed. Puffy rust-colored blots with hair mixed in. Underneath the clouds, a mountain had taken shape. Aspen trees in the foreground. Moonbeams. Pinpoints of light illuminating the night sky. In the course of an hour, a full-on AbEx evening landscape had emerged.

After the piece was complete, Barrantine went inside, took a shower, sobered up a bit with a pot of coffee and headed back to Denver. His focus was sharp. Nerves raw. Delving into the spirit of Pollock had stimulated a new idea, the final piece of the counseling puzzle.

Barrantine turned into a driveway, walked up a set of

wooden steps and rang the doorbell. A dog barked. A tall figure shuffled toward the door and peered through the keyhole.
After a pause, the door handle started to move.

57 – Downtown

Ana placed the last few items of clothing in her overnight bag. Marie would be picking her up soon for the Fourth of July celebration on the 16th Street Mall. Marie felt it would be a nice getaway for Ana; she could let down her hair a little bit and set aside thoughts of Martin, even if just for an evening.

When they arrived at the hotel, they quickly dropped off their suitcases. "I'm glad we are doing this," said Marie, staring at the humongous book that lay on the hotel bed. "But I'm not sure we will have any time for reading."

"I know. I brought it along just in case."

Marie felt like she was getting a workout when she picked up the copy of David Foster Wallace's *Infinite Jest*.

"This is a beast."

"Actually, my counselor suggested it. He told me it might help me get in touch with my wild side."

Marie laughed.

"So, your counselor wants you to get in touch with your wild side? I'm thinking you are seeing the right counselor. Not sure about the book, though. Where should we go?"

"Let's just walk."

"Sounds perfect."

Ana and Marie skipped down Blake Street, first stopping at the Rio Grande, where they could chase down an order of chips and guac with a margarita.

"I'm so happy it's not raining," said Marie. "What a crappy summer it has been."

"Totally," said Ana, already feeling the effects of the tequila after a few sips.

"So, back to your wild side," said Marie. "Waiter, two shots of tequila please and the check."

"Marie! I'm not even half way through my first."

"Oh, come on, we are going to live a little."

The tequila shots arrived.

"Bottoms up."

When the booze hit Ana's bloodstream, the restaurant started to spin. Green parrot-shaped piñatas swung in the periphery. Glasses tilted to the side. The conversation started to flow. Single lady, non-married topics were discussed. The type of jeans a man wears. Whether he is heavy or lean, or has a beard. And if he has a beard, does it add or detract when he goes down there. Ana hadn't talked like this for years. The laughing. The uncensored conversation, her words taking on a slightly forbidden quality.

"So, what are you going to do when a man offers to buy you a drink?" said Marie.

"Depends on the man."

"You better say yes!"

"I'll consider it."

"Are you ready to head to the dance club?"

"Let's go!"

58 – Boom Boom Room

The crystal ball at the Boom Boom Room spun like a gyroscope. Wall-to-wall people. Smashed bodies glistening with sweat. Women wore tight-fitting jeans or short skirts, clothes to make a man's mind go feral. Men presented stylishly. Short hair. Cologne. Black leather belts, shiny buckles. Silk shirts. Bulging muscles. Ana hadn't danced hip-hop in years. But the mood felt right, open, just as it should be. Jay-Z and Kanye were playing "No Church in the Wild." Her hips swished from side to side, in and out, squares, triangles, octagons, every geometrical shape. Men circled, made figure eights around her, changing her into a cubist painting. *Girl with a Mandolin.* Ana's body tingled. Dual grinding, one in front, the other in back, sandwiched. She felt loose. Thoughts flying, drinks flowing, the Boom Boom Room lived up to its name.

A Latin man with pointy boots, denim jeans and smooth skin held a vodka tonic in his hand. "Would you like?" he asked.

Ana grabbed the drink and fell into his arms. Now mixing liquors, her senses intermingled like she had synesthesia. The Latin lover's brown skin. The tartness of the lime in the vodka. His firm, soft hands when they touched her hips. The back of her neck tingled. Everything tasted or smelled or looked like something else. A tunnel of wind blew through the Boom Boom Room.

When the song finished, Javier grabbed Ana's hand, brought her to the sidelines where his friend, Marco, was entangled with Marie. The conversation was light and suave, the perfect combination of words, laughing, in-the-moment small talk.

Ana thought about Martin. *Is this what he feels?* But the question was quickly blown apart by the muscular thighs and bleached jeans of Javier. Besides, *this* is what Martin had always wanted. Wild Ana. Free Ana. Ana who would grind and contort. Her drink spilled on her own shirt when she straddled Javier's thigh and fell backwards. Javier grabbed Ana's drink, set it on a table and led her out to the dance floor.

They danced for another hour. Javier's moves and jokes softened her up, made her breath heavy, want to lose control, enter an alternate reality. The Zen of drinking and dancing. The allure of Javier's length. Of his Latin lightness. Of fun. Of simplicity. Of Ana's own Sea and Sky. Her body wet, hair disheveled.

Marie watched Javier's moves from the sidelines like they were part of a paid performance or an audition. She could see Ana's essence disappear into his arms. Peachy, soft, glossy, Ana's eyes glowed of liberation and libation, encouraged by recklessness, while Javier nibbled on her ear. "You have a beautiful smile," he said, "and your hips are perfect for Latin dancing. Did you ever live in Latin America? You move with such grace."

Javier's hand rested on Ana's lower back. He led her out of the bar. Every few steps, his hand would slide down, pull Ana's skirt up slightly, her pink lace underwear glowing in the night like a neon side blinking stop and go. As they got in the car, she fell across the seat barely conscious, kissing Javier's neck, rubbing his chest and stomach as he drove.

When they entered Javier's apartment, she fell to her back on the bed. Like he had been invited to a party, Javier was ready for the moment. He pulled Ana's skirt down, lifted her shirt over her head, unclipped her bra and began to suck on her breasts. She tingled, moaned and reached for the top button of his pants.

Ping.

The button broke off. Ana spread her legs and pulled him in. Javier followed her lead, clutching her thighs, pressing them out as far as he could to achieve full penetration, teasing her with lengthy circles, in and out, stronger, harder, varied rhythms, high-pitched sounds. Powerful gusts of wind. Sleet. A bit of hail. Ana screamed out like she had been struck by a bolt of lightning in the rain.

59 – Ana's Dream

Ana awoke the next morning to a pounding headache. As if she had been pummeled by a wave and bounced along the sandy bottom, her entire body hurt. She stepped out of bed, walked to the bathroom, filled up a cup and swallowed two aspirin. Ana scanned the hotel room. She was alone. No Javier. No Marie. How did she get back to the hotel last night? She couldn't remember.

Dizzy, she fell to the mattress, her emotions tumbling as she recalled her dream from the night before. A woman with jet-black hair rode a mustang by the sea. The woman's pupils were fire-red. Her teeth bone-white. Diamonds, hot to touch, glistened on the same beach she and Martin had gotten married at. Sharp rocks jutted from the sea. Crabs scurried across the sand. Broken sand dollars. A green flash as the sun sunk into the sea.

In the dream, Ana found herself swimming to shore in a desperate attempt to make it to a hillside so she could hide in the bushes. Her legs were scratched; blood dripped from her shins. The dark woman on the mustang, now stomach-deep in the sea, scanned the hillside. Ana crouched under a tree, covering her face so the witch didn't notice the whites of her eyes.

When the aspirin finally took effect, Ana sat up and scanned the room. Her clothes were strewn across the floor. She was naked. Her whole body hurt. *Everywhere.* Now more aware of how she really felt, Ana limped over to the mirror. Anxiety kicked in. Not just in relation to having sex with a total stranger, but the way in which she prepared for it. Never before had Ana fully shaved herself. Not even when Martin had requested it on his birthday. Ana touched her stomach. Did

Javier wear protection? She couldn't remember. Maybe there was a mention of a condom; maybe there wasn't.

"*What if I am pregnant?*" a silent voice cried out.

When she left the mirror, images from her dream came back. The witch now rode the mustang to the outer break, and Ana's legs were tangled with an octopus while she hid in the bushes. Waves touched her toes. She shook with fear, tried to look invisible as the witch scanned the hillside. When waves finally engulfed the witch and the mustang, Ana felt tension release in her chest. The octopus let go of her legs. The sky went dark. The witch faded away. And Ana wondered if she had been touched by a darkness much greater than herself.

60 – Another Woman

Martin set up his food truck outside Rickolis Brewery in Wheat Ridge. Although the past two nights saw an uptick in business, it was a Monday night and there were no customers, so he stepped inside the brewery to grab a beer. Sitting down at the bar, Martin was served by the owner, Rick, who was riding high after winning a GABF gold medal for his Statik Barley wine. Although Martin considered ordering something lighter, he couldn't resist tasting the award-winning 13% beer, the dense hops and caramel coating his mouth like agave nectar over peaches.

The beer went down quickly. What's next? With no orders on the food truck, why not have another? "What do you recommend, Rick? How's the Black Pline?"

"Well, at 9.5%, it's a real quaffer next to the Statik," he joked.

Martin took a gulp of beer. The door to the brewery swung open. A woman with red hair strolled in.

"Is anyone sitting here?" she asked.

"No, please sit down," said Martin, scooting his chair over.

Rick asked the woman what she was having. The woman looked at Martin.

"Any recommendations?"

"The Black Pline is great, and I'd recommend the Statik. Both are big, hoppy beers."

"I like big and hoppy. I'll go for the Statik," she said. "Hi, my name is Jen. Do you live around here?"

"Hi Jen. I'm Martin. I actually live in River North. I operate the food truck outside."

"Cool. Must be a fun job." Jen touched Martin's forearm and

slid her hand down to the One-Impulse Time Machine. "Nice watch. Is it for fitness?"

"No, it's just a watch. I'm borrowing it at the moment. Actually, the battery is dying." Martin reached down and shut it off. "I should probably get back to work here soon."

Jen looked outside. "No one's in line. Why don't you have one more. It's on me. And then I'd like to order food." Jen touched Martin's forearm again. This time the touch was heavier, more dialed into the moment, into the Zen of drinking high alcohol beers. Two minds. Two pints. Two bodies becoming one.

"Twist my arm."

"Okay, I will!" Jen bent Martin's arm behind his back.

"Ouch."

They laughed.

"So are you gonna be able to cook after these beers?" asked Jen.

"I don't know, but I've got an important customer I'd like to satisfy."

"I'm sure I will love what you give me."

The conversation took on sexual overtones, and Martin fidgeted with the One-Impulse Time Machine.

"So, are you from Colorado?" asked Jen.

"Seattle," said Martin. "But I've traveled a lot."

"Me, too. Any big adventures recently?"

"Not really, and you?"

"I did a thirty-mile hike through the Bechler area of Yellowstone Park last summer."

"No way," said Martin. "I worked in the Park years ago myself, and I hiked the Bechler. Did you visit the backcountry hot springs?"

"You mean Mr. Bubbles?"

"Yeah, that's the one."

"Of course," said Jen, winking.

"And how long have you been in Denver?" asked Martin.

"Around five years."

"Do you like it?"

"It's cool. I mean, it's not Wyoming-cool, but I love the nature-culture mix."

A few customers entered Rickolis.

"Looks like I better man the food truck," said Martin. "What would you like?"

"Surprise me," said Jen.

Martin walked back to the food truck and wondered how he could surprise her. A line formed. He would have to think quickly. He could make his three favorite tacos, and what if he wrote his phone number on a napkin? What would it hurt? Might as well follow Barrantine's advice about exploring, taking risks. Jen was just another one of those risks, another step in the counseling, another way to grow as a person, to discover his true feelings. The alcohol did not mince words on these points.

Martin assembled the tacos and brought them over to the bar. "Bye," he said, placing his hand on Jen's shoulder. "I enjoyed meeting you."

Jen unfolded the napkin, blew Martin a kiss—a kiss that flew through the brewery like a fairy on a rogue wave.

White sequins popped off the fairy's dress.

The kiss landed on Martin's cheek.

He stepped into his food truck, scanned the One-Impulse Time Machine as if he was ready to use it. But what was he doing? What was he thinking? It was too late to push the button, too late to turn back the clock. The momentum was already in full swing. The window to his own past pushed wide open.

Skateboard in his hand. Wind blowing through the streets of Seattle. Memories bouncing back-and-forth. Hippocampus to thalamus. Present to past.

> *Time to lube up the trucks before Mom comes home.*
> *Gotta run, gotta hide, gotta roam.*
> *Ain't no point staying, listening to the sounds.*
> *Ain't no point pretending we in bounds.*

61 – Zeke Follows the Pain Molecules

Zeke, Desmond and the rest of the Diver Neurons followed the trail of blood left by the sperm whale. Reckoning they were a day behind the great beast, the scout team moved through the viscous water with caution, taking careful note of the high concentrations of pain molecules suspended in the ocean brine. Hoping to rediscover their normal state of being so they could pursue mermaid pussy for pussy's sake, everyone was on high alert, searching for new clues to help them unlock the mystery.

"You think this is because of Banshee?" asked Zeke.

"You mean the blood? Not sure," replied Desmond. "The only one who might know is gone."

"You talking 'bout Chuck?"

"Yep."

Zeke fiddled with a dreadlock.

Meanwhile, Banshee's screams grew louder and the pain molecules changed character. Bigger. Bulkier. Suggestive of greater suffering, they trended upward to the surface of the Sea, where the sun illuminated their internal structure, revealing a venous heart-shaped core.

"Look," said Desmond. "See that dark piece of real estate to the left. I believe that's an island. I think we're actually heading for the center of a bay."

Sure enough, some ten fathoms below the surface of the Sea, the tides changed, and the water churned in a kind of savage convection, suggesting a landlocked part of the marine world. A bloody whirlpool formed. Screams intensified. A battle raged. One creature fighting for its life against another. The scout team swam closer. Just as they had suspected, the sperm whale was being attacked, dismembered by a wicked creature, cannibalized for mere pleasure.

Sensing she was being watched, Banshee pulled her head from the loins of the whale and panned to the Diver Neurons, straight at Zeke.

"You silly little bitch," she laughed, her black cape wafting back-and-forth. "You dumb little fuck. Well, that was hardly a fuck with your tiny penis and all."

Banshee extracted her obsidian claws from the sperm whale's intestines and swam straight at the Diver Neurons. Now only thirty feet away, she started to dance. Nasty, wicked, her fingers folded into her cape like she was touching herself. But this was different. The masturbation, that is. Unwomanly to be precise, her hands cupped in a circle, knuckles taut like they were holding a stick shift. Banshee laughed, pulled up her cape.

What in the blue Jesus?

The luscious orange sea sponge that they dipped their wicks into only three months earlier had vanished.

In its place a gangly, brown, half-hard set of cock and balls stared them in the face. Banshee let go of her penis and moved her hand to the back side. She bent over, pushed her middle finger into her own glory hole, while her index finger prospected the rim of her anus like an astronaut landing on the moon. And at that moment, the horror had crystalized. Banshee was not the hot-bodied woman they had supposed. No, Banshee was a tranny, and Zeke and the other Diver Neurons now realized that they had sex with her ass.

62 – Martin and Jen Go Hiking

Martin had always struggled to understand what he wanted in a woman. *Really wanted.* What would sustain him, allow him to be both satisfied and good. Was it order? Stability? Routine? Or was it the opposite? An unbridled woman who could fully relax, unwind, let down her hair?

Order or chaos?

Apollo or Dionysus?

Of course, he wanted both, but like a round-square, not everything is possible within a single being, not every mode of existence makes sense. And as he hiked up to Eaglesmere Lakes with Jen, the questions took on a new kind of force. A pressure in his internal core. A desire to explore himself in concrete terms. Empirically. Soberly. Without the time travel watch. Within the context of a clear Weather System, and a woman who was in many ways Ana's feminine opposite.

Turns out, Jen was an artist who made a living as a healthcare aide. Prior to this, she went to film school in New York City where she worked a stint as an actress making low-budget films. Drugs followed. Hard drugs. Then rehab. Eventually Jen pulled herself together, but the wild side never went away, and Martin could sense it in the way she walked, talked and dressed. Her tight green shorts, nipply white t-shirt. Puffy lips slathered in high-end gloss that popped like a balloon when her mouth moved.

Jen followed Martin over a creek crossing. Their pace was fast, unnaturally fast. Sexual energy pervaded the forest. In the grasses and the plants. On the wings of the birds and the bees and the Aspen trees. Jen asked Martin about his relationship status, and Martin explained the separation, which turned her on.

"You don't mind, do you?" she asked, unclipping her bra and placing it in her backpack. "I'm hot."

This was the sort of woman Martin watched porn for. "Not at all," he said, smiling.

Now at the halfway point of their hike, they sat down for lunch. Martin made chicken sandwiches with fresh spinach, tomatoes, swish cheese and pesto mayo.

"I hope you like it," he said.

"Love it," said Jen stretching backwards, showing off her marvelous chest.

"So, have you been with anyone since you've been separated?" she asked.

"No, not really."

Jen placed her hand on Martin's thigh. "Do you want to be with someone?"

Martin nodded. "Of course."

But his sexual drive was not what he expected, and oddly enough, Martin's parents were on his mind—specifically what brought them together as a couple. Did they love each other? Like each other? Hard to say. So much of Martin's youth felt like an abstraction, or a dirty window, his mother hardly a mother, his father less than zero.

Must have been the animal in them, he thought. The sharing in each other's vices. Temporal pleasures. Darkness. Strong winds. Hail. A pretense of togetherness. An accident named Martin, who they would need to support until he was eighteen.

He leaned over, kissed Jen.

She dropped her sandwich, dug her fingernails into his back. Martin lifted her shirt and started massaging her breasts.

Jen moaned.

Sensing she was the type of woman who could orgasm quickly, Martin tried to slow the pace. Not ready to take this to completion, he leaned back, sandwich in the air. "Should we eat lunch?"

"I see how you are," said Jen, writing Martin off as a patient type. "We can eat first."

After lunch, they continued up the trial to Eaglesmere Lakes, and Martin felt increasingly uneasy, full of guilt. Though he was separated, free from apparent obligation, there was resistance, a sense that his principles ran in a straight line with no spaces in between. And the prior thoughts about his mother and father dangled in the air like a wet blanket covered with snow.

When they arrived at the lake, Jen started coming on to Martin again. They kissed. She rubbed his chest and shoulders, moaned like a cat in heat, ready to go as far as he wanted. At first, Martin tried to roll with it, test himself, maybe take this to completion. After all, if this was really *him*, why not finalize the separation now? There would be less hurt in the end. Ana deserved at least this.

Martin pulled away.

"I guess I'm not ready for this," he said.

"Whatever," responded Jen, clearly frustrated. "Did I make a mistake?"

"No, it's not you, it's me. I'm just a little off from my separation, you know?"

Jen acted as if she understood, but when they arrived at the car, the passion of the hike was deflated. The fact they didn't have sex, didn't engage in any high-level petting, seemed to place their relationship, even if only platonic, on a road to nowhere. In the end, Martin wanted the intimacy to be more challenging. He wanted to struggle to feel the other's inner workings. Perhaps at that moment, he wanted to be different from his mother and father, to view their relationship for what it really was, for what it could have been.

Martin stepped out of his car, grabbed his backpack and entered his condo.

Or maybe he entered an unconscious threshold of his own mind.

When he stepped inside, the house seemed half empty. Raw feelings dangled from the walls. Principles were scattered here and there. By the electric fireplace. Between the stove and the cabinet. On the corner of the desk, where a five-year service award, a pen set to be precise, sat beside a stack of early period *Aquaman* comics. His favorite superhero growing up, Aquaman was king of the marine world, master of the ocean blue. And when Martin was a young boy building sand castles on the beaches outside Seattle, he imagined that he, too, was an oceanic superhero, a famous steward of the sea.

Martin blew dust off a 1965 copy of *Trap of the Sinister Sea Nymphs* and turned to a random page. He couldn't really remember what the theme of the comic was, couldn't recall where he got it, but somehow the story still lived inside him, and he wondered why.

Why do we sense things we can't remember, feel things we can't recall?

Martin took off his glasses, wiped his eyes.

Is there anything in our experience that ever goes away, anything that doesn't matter?

Pipes creaked.

A black hornet tapped on the window screen.

Why do questions multiply when answers are given?

Do any of us know what kind of odyssey we've been on?

63 – Nate Goes Under

Two days had passed since Jonk-Q Mosileeleelee's visit with Nate, and Banshee still feasted on the sperm whale in the cove. The sight was disturbing, savage really—a sickening red bouillabaisse of torn cartilage, scraps of muscle and bone. Each time the sperm whale rolled over in agony, Banshee would bury her head into the great beast's innards, screaming out in sadistic pleasure, slapping her black-caped arms on the surface of the water to show dominance.

Nate placed his dive gear over his shoulders, attached his regulator to his mouth and prepared to enter the Sea. Although the scene was terrifying, he tried to focus on Jonk-Q's advice about embracing uncertainty and carrying out the mission of the explorer. Nate placed his flippers in the red foam and walked along the shallow pools below the cliff. When the waves became too strong for him to stand, and the wails of Banshee grew more distinct, he knew it was time to enter the ocean blue. Taking a deep breath, he surveyed the horizon and took the plunge.

Splash!

His body sank into the fifty-degree water.

At first the temperature was jarring, and Nate felt claustrophobic, the sounds of his own breath squeezing tight like he was trapped in a cave. But when his nerves started to settle, he realized he was more buoyant than expected. Swimming had a more relaxed quality; the water seemed tranquil. The deeper he descended into the salty brine, the more he started to feel in control, the more he accepted his own fate.

But what was his fate? At the moment, Nate's fate seemed bound up with his father's. Odd as it might sound, given their obvious differences in religious orientation, Nate felt a curious affinity for his father, almost as if they were identical people. He felt it in the purity of their search, in the uncompromising nature of their lives. He felt it in his journey to the Sea and in Pastor Samuel's lifelong search for God. Although they were worlds apart in distance, they seemed aligned in spirit, their futures connected in ways he could only sense.

Nate swam toward the carcass of the sperm whale, toward Banshee, toward the very essence of mystery itself. Now 200 meters away from the wailing beast, the water suddenly cleared, and Nate noticed Banshee's obsidian claws slicing through the water. Her back was turned, so he swam closer to investigate Banshee's line of sight. Hoping the savage creature would not notice, Nate extracted an underwater light from his backpack and tracked the source of her gaze.

In the far distance, a group of cells vibrated in the water. The cells were hard to make out entirely, but Nate noticed that their bodies were like his. At the center of each one was a colorful nucleus. Around the nucleus, blond, brunette, red and black dendrites wafted back-and-forth. Each cell had a thick myelin sheath protecting it from the cold. Along their axon endings, fingers and toes protruded. Even their mannerisms and movements suggested that the cells were conversing with each other and had a social nature. Nate turned off his flashlight and contemplated his next move. Although these creatures presented risk, there appeared to be no other options. He would need to make contact.

64 – After a Wild Night

Ana's face looked like a cliff with fresh cracks. Barrantine knew she was not well. Naturally, he worried if David Foster Wallace was to blame. Perhaps Ana had read the book, or large parts of it, only later to discover the author's fate. Perhaps she regarded *Infinite Jest* as a cruel joke. Yet when Ana explained what had happened on the Fourth of July with Javier—that she felt like she had cheated on Martin, that she could be pregnant and did not know who she was—Barrantine experienced a sense of relief, even though he realized his strongest work as a counselor must lie ahead.

"Ana, I realize this was out of character for you, but in my view, you did not cheat on Martin. When there is infidelity in a marriage, and when there is a corresponding separation, I believe this amounts to a kind of moral severing of the greater marital commitment. I think that's the first thing to understand—legally you are still married, morally you are not. And you are only human. We all experiment. We all make choices we regret. But this regret, if you want to call it that, is not all bad."

Ana wiped a tear away from her cheek. "Okay."

"So the original idea from our prior session involved letting go. And I believe you did let go, which is amazing, but I suppose this does come with its own challenges, its own risks and rewards, which is all a part of it. Yet the very practice of letting go is itself part of the solution, and I don't want you to lose sight of the fact that you can use this to help you going forward."

"How so?"

"Well, one thing you have clearly demonstrated is that you

are free, or, you know, free in a conventional sense."

Ana rolled her eyes. Barrantine immediately recognized he was over-intellectualizing.

"What I mean," he continued, "is that you can do anything you want, be any kind of person you desire. In other words, you are not constrained by the past, and you truly are your own person. On top of this, in terms of the future, perhaps you can use this event to help understand Martin. Of course, Martin does not deserve any sympathy or have any kind an excuse for his behavior, but this type of experience can simply help bridge any potential gaps, if that makes sense."

Ana scratched her knuckle in frustration. Questions hammered her from all directions. Was Barrantine the right counselor for her? And the stupid David Foster Wallace book, which was difficult read and had no obvious application to her life. And, for Christ's sake, the One-Sentence Time Machine. Where was all this really going?

"You know, the truth is this does make me feel sympathy for Martin, which I hate. I hate feeling bad for someone who has cheated on me because I was incapable of letting go. That makes me feel like shit, actually."

Barrantine turned away.

"And you know what else," continued Ana. "I feel bad for the regret he must feel...regret for cheating on me, when, in all reality, maybe it made sense. I hate all that because I don't think he deserves it."

"I would agree, of course," said Barrantine, nodding.

Ana picked up her purse and stood up. "I need to call it early today. I don't feel like talking. I'll call you later to set up another appointment." Ana slammed the door shut. "Or not."

65 – Barrantine's Summation

Two in the afternoon. Barrantine was drinking red wine earlier than usual. The pressure to make a difference, to correct his own deficiencies, to help rekindle Ana and Martin's marriage, and bring them to the place from which change is possible, pressed upon his psyche. To be clear, Barrantine believed Martin and Ana were good for each other. He believed in the confluence of their histories. He believed their struggles could be turned into strengths, that their responses to counseling were grounded in the authentic spirit of change.

Reminding himself that a counselor must follow through on his methodologies, maintain consistency and avoid too much avant-garde jazz, Barrantine recalled the painful day at the cabin when he was brought to his knees by his own mistakes. The flippant, ill-considered advice to read *Infinite Jest*. The failure to embrace radical subjectivity in his practice. His clinical, scientific approach to matters of the heart. And even his own metaphors. Opening up the windows on your house? Letting go? *Really*.

Hoping the whole experience had truly helped him breakdown the borders of his own self, he picked up a pen and began to summarize his findings:

• The essence of Martin and Ana's relationship is one of trying to complete each other in relation to differences in their being, anchored in childhood trauma and undergirded by certain mysterious, inaccessible parts of the psyche.

• Ana experienced a more black and white upbringing in which discipline and control were paramount. Her father's being a mathematician suggests this. Martin was overexposed to many shades of grey, never learning proper boundaries.

• Martin has a turbulent spirit, characterized by a propensity for overabundance. Ana is controlled, more apt to suppress her desires.

• Because of his overabundance, Martin desires more control and order in certain respects. Ana wants more freedom, the embracing of chaos.

• Martin's life journey involves a struggle with convention. Ana has a greater tendency to embrace convention.

• Martin's occupation is a response to his shadow via the pain of being disconnected from his father and the desire to leave his mother. Ana's occupation is a response to her shadow via finding job security and enjoyment through her work.

• Ana's struggle is to allow impulses to surface. Martin's struggle is to subtract or subdue them.

• Martin's challenge is one of channeling his impulses to align with the moral. Ana's challenge is one of allowing her impulses to surface as a challenge to the moral.

• Although they appear to be moving in different directions, both needed to move away from each other before they moved back together. Both needed outside experiences to solidify their feelings for each other, whatever those feelings might be.

• Ana's suffering and her compensation structures involving order, convention, stability and control are grounded in her father's suicide. Martin's issues of regulative control are anchored in his mother's alcoholism, in the emotional instability and intensity of both parents.

• Both Martin and Ana are governed by the same mechanism governing everyone—a biological/genetic causal chain reaching back many generations.

• Both are governed by quantum randomness and its effects on consciousness.

• Both want a release from life's suffering, but have not found healthy ways to do so. Martin's hypersexuality has brought him a lot of pain in his life. Ana's anxiety and depression have at times been debilitating.

• In summary, the challenges are clear, as is the route to a solution. It's time to proceed to the final phase of counseling.

66 – Reintroduction

The sky was aqua blue, the sun a scintillating globe. It was August, and though the wind blew hard, the Great Storm of Denver, which raged for five months, had finally broken. Martin felt lighter as he hopped up the stairs to Barrantine's office. When he arrived, the door was cracked open. He peeked in.

"Come in, come in," said Barrantine, legs propped up on the desk. Dressed in a lightweight mesh fishing shirt and cargo shorts, he was more casual than usual. His hair was messy, without style.

"Did you have a nice vacation?" asked Martin, noticing the change in Barrantine's demeanor.

"Yes, the time away at the cabin was rejuvenating, and important professionally."

"Great, glad to hear it. Very glad to hear it."

Fifteen minutes passed before any real words were said. Although disappointed, Martin wondered if Barrantine was having personal issues himself, or perhaps he was mailing it in as a counselor. We all have off days.

Then came a knock on the door.

"Come in," said Barrantine.

Ana walked in. When she saw Martin, she lost grip on her purse.

"Please, sit down," said Barrantine.

Martin moved over on the couch.

Ana gave Barrantine a piercing look. "I didn't know Martin would be here."

"I didn't either," said Martin, whose heart beat in his throat.

"Yes, well, I'm sure you are both surprised that I invited you here today, and perhaps even a tad angry with me." Barrantine sipped green tea from an unglazed pottery cup. "Which I completely understand. There were so many things I asked you to trust in the counseling process—the separate sessions, the consideration of technology, the introduction of new technology, the potentially unpredictable effects of counseling itself." Barrantine rubbed his temples. "But I am here to ask you to trust me one last time.

"So, I have been seeing you now individually for a while, and I recently came to the conclusion that reintroduction is necessary. But I want you to know that the post-separation sessions were not the plan all along. Rather, your relationship simply evolved in this way. You have both been down difficult paths for the last few months. I now believe your paths have converged and you have arrived at the place from which change is possible."

Barrantine paged through his notes and drawings, stopping on a sketch from an early session—a bed with long wooden legs elevated high in the sky. The piece seemed unfinished, so he reached in his desk drawer and grabbed a carrot orange colored pencil. "Give me a second," he said, sketching a long duvet that hung from the bed.

"When I first saw you," Barrantine continued, "there were issues with how you wanted to spend your leisure time—Fridays, for example. There were issues with intimacy, with texting, with trust in general. What I have now concluded is that you are two souls trying to complete each other in ways connected to your upbringing, to your past as a whole. This is a powerful bond that you have in common. Not all couples have such a strong undercurrent to their relationship."

Martin and Ana were silent. Wind gusts shook the windows. Trees blew from side to side.

"Ana, your father's death had a profound effect on you, as it would on anyone. And yet, prior to this, there were significant challenges in your upbringing. The passive-aggressive nature of your parents' relationship with each other, for example. The myriad feelings lurking beneath the surface. Your father's depression. Martin, you likewise experienced profound difficulties in your own past, including your father's alcoholism and the erratic absentee nature of your mother in particular. I would also suggest there was frustration, perhaps even unresolved anger toward your father, for not taking certain steps that you, as younger man, thought he should take."

Barrantine closed his notebook. "So now we move to the present, where you each have amazing traits to offer the other—traits related to your past as a whole, to your own unique forms of suffering in particular. But these traits do not always come easy, nor do they mesh in real time. Hence, the counseling."

A long pause. Only Mazzy's purr could be heard.

"As I have surmised, one of you has turbulent impulses. The other has impulses that have been suppressed. The challenge is to realize these impulses together, to make them work in complementary ways. But to do this, several steps must be taken. The spending of quality time with each other is one. Managing technology is another. Then there is Martin's new job, which strikes me as a step in the right direction. Ana, were you aware that Martin purchased a food truck?"

Ana leaned on Martin, placing her hand on his knee. "I had no idea. Really? I think that's amazing."

"You do?"

Barrantine glanced at his watch. Time moved quickly, and the session had already finished.

"I think we are going to need more time today," he said. "Ana, Martin, can you stay for a while longer?"

They nodded.

"Great, let's take a five-minute break. In the meantime, why don't you take a gander at this. I think you will find it interesting." Barrantine handed Martin a newspaper clipping.

He read the headline.

Martin James Saves Ballard Tigers

67 – Nate Meets His Fate

Nate calibrated the regulator on his dive tanks. Two hours of oxygen remained, which should be enough time to make contact with the Diver Neurons, but he would need to move quickly. His strategy was simple. Follow the large blood halo surrounding Banshee until he reached the other side of the cove. Once on the other side, assess the situation and approach the Diver Neurons. Ideally, the blood halo would camouflage him, keep him out of Banshee's line of sight, at least until he had made it to the other side.

Nate started the long arc around the bay. At first, swimming was difficult, as the tide moved against him. But when he reached the outer break, the tide changed character, and a current pulled him in the direction he wanted to go. With surprisingly little effort, Nate was swept to the opposite side of the bay and could now see several hundred thousand Diver Neurons congregating.

Nate treaded water in a calm spot and checked his regulator. An hour and a half remained. But how should he approach the Diver Neurons? Make a loud noise? Use a certain hand gesture? How would they interpret his communication once he made contact?

Ultimately, Nate decided on the straightforward route. He would simply swim over to the Diver Neurons, introduce himself and hope for the best. Checking his regulator one last time, he began his approach. Swimming as calmly as possible, he moved toward a group of neurons who were huddled together.

Desmond heard a splash in the water and looked up. "What in the hell? What is that little guy?"

Zeke placed his hand on his dive knife.

Nate swam closer, now twenty feet away.

Now ten feet away.

Nate was upon them.

"Hello," he said, extending his hand.

Desmond eyeballed Zeke. Zeke eyeballed Desmond.

"Hello," said Desmond back, shaking Nate's hand.

Nate gestured to the cloud of blood in the water. "Is that normal down here?"

"Down here? No, it's not normal," responded Desmond.

"And the sound?" asked Nate, referring to the piercing wail of Banshee.

"None of this is normal. Our home has been corrupted."

"Corrupted by what?" asked Nate.

Zeke leaned over and whispered in Desmond's ear. "You think we can trust this dude?"

"Your guess is as good as mine," said Desmond, "but what do we have to lose? Plus, he's outnumbered by the millions and doesn't look real tough."

Desmond stared hard into Nate's dive mask.

"We're not sure. We think the Sea has been corrupted by what we did. We think we might have had relations with the wrong mermaid."

"Relations?" he asked.

Zeke stepped in. "We think we might have diddled the wrong ho. Know what I'm sayin?"

"Kind of," said Nate.

"Well, she ugly now," continued Zeke, as if to defend his sexual choice, "but she didn't used to be. She used to be a hot-ass, smooth-skinned, pink-lipstick-wearing hoochie koo, with an oak-town booty that went on for days before we first tapped that ass."

Nate adjusted his regulator. "Sounds like a moral issue," he said clearing his throat, "with tapping that ass."

"Moral issue?" asked Zeke. "Moral" was not a word in the Diver Neuron vocabulary.

Nate could see the blank stares. "Never mind."

"So, where you come from?" asked Zeke.

"Up there," said Nate. "I came from the Sky, above the Storm?"

"Huh?"

"Yeah, I live above the clouds."

"No shit," Desmond chimed in. "I guess that's why you're wearing the metal tanks."

"Yeah, I can't breathe underwater."

"What are you doing down here then?" asked Desmond.

"I'm exploring. This is the first time anyone of my kind has ever visited the Sea."

Desmond scratched his head.

"So, maybe you can help us with our situation?" he asked.

"I have a feeling that's why I'm here," said Nate.

"All right, should we take this conversation elsewhere? How deep can you go with that equipment on?"

"About 200 fathoms, but I only have an hour."

"Sure, no problem, we'll be quick. Follow me."

Nate followed Desmond, Zeke and other Diver Neurons into the ocean blue where they searched for a cave to escape Banshee's screams.

68 – Goodbye

When Barrantine returned from the restroom, he walked over to his bookshelf and grabbed a folder that held sketches from a number of his inventions. The One-Sentence and One-Impulse Time Machine diagrams were there, along with a couple of defunct creations grounded in bringing more humor and seriousness into people's lives. He also purchased two manila envelopes, one with Martin's name written on it.

"Before we talk about what is in these envelopes and the newspaper clipping you are holding, I'd like to say a few words." Barrantine fiddled with his shirt pocket. "I'd like to apologize," he said. "Apologize for making some real mistakes. Yes, it's true, there were successes, but overall, I believe I have been unable to complete my practice, to find a proper capstone to the counseling, to give couples like yourselves the necessary tools to complete their journeys."

Ana noticed Barrantine's voice started to crack, and despite her own sense of betrayal, she assured him that he'd been an excellent counselor.

"You're too kind, Ana, too kind. Yet I need to be able to say these things to you both." Barrantine lit an old candle, placed it between them. The smell of juniper and pine. A thin plume of smoke wafted through the air. "I have been too impersonal," he said, "too clinical, too focused on inventing instead of listening. Further, certain of my methods have been half-baked, and I have misused metaphors. In terms of my general approach, while I have advocated taking certain risks, I don't believe I myself have taken some of those same risks."

Barrantine handed the manila envelope to Martin. "Please look inside."

Martin shuffled through the contents. Letters. Old mementos. More newspaper clippings...from basketball of all things.

Martin James Nets 16.

Trojans: 12-0. Martin James MVP.

"What?"

"Keep looking," said Barrantine. "There's more."

Martin scanned a stack of photos from the folder. A picture of he and his father standing in front of the polar bear exhibit at the Denver Zoo. Another at the entrance to Elitches. More basketball pics. Action shots of Martin making a layup, shooting the three, running down the court for a fast break jumper. Martin wore a medal around his neck. His father's arm was draped over his shoulder.

"Your dad told me you were a really good basketball player."

"What?" said Martin.

"I stopped by his house. I hope you don't mind. After my vacation up at the cabin, I felt compelled to pay your father a visit."

"How did you find out where he lived?"

Barrantine gestured to Ana.

"I told him," she said. "I hope you don't mind."

"But...I *wasn't* a good basketball player."

"I'm afraid that's not quite right, Martin. According to your father, you were an excellent player with a wonderful spirit. The photos and the newspaper clippings speak for themselves. Alonzo told me the whole story about when you quit playing basketball and started skateboarding. Not that there is anything wrong with skateboarding, but he said this happened after your mother didn't let you move to Denver."

"True, but it's not like he did much about it. Why didn't he try a little harder? Why did he stop calling?"

Barrantine rubbed his hands together. "Your father admitted a lot of mistakes. He said he got depressed when you couldn't move out. He said he lost the restaurant and ended up homeless, just as you had suspected."

"But how can I not remember a lot of this?"

The candle sitting in front of them leaked wax from its side.

"Memories are strange," said Barrantine, "especially when we are young, and especially when trauma is involved. In this way, they are pliable, and they can act as a kind of defense mechanism, if that makes sense. Sometimes we're not ready for our own memories, and they need to play out in the shadow world, unconsciously."

Crackling sounds from the candle. The metal attached to the wick was exposed. The bottom liquefied.

"And there's one more thing," said Barrantine, who reached across the desk and handed Martin a yellow sheet of paper. "Your father wanted me to make sure you read this. He said he wrote it shortly after he lost the restaurant. He said he was ashamed to give it to you because it wasn't any good. By the way, I disagree with this. I actually found the poem quite poignant. Please give it a read."

69 – Regret

I messed myself up, Son,
but I don't want that to happen to you.
I went down to the Denver,
tried to press on through.
Son, I've been living through the ups and downs of life,
been flying on a wing and a prayer.
But you the best thing I've known,
make me breath better than air.
Son, if I could turn back the clock and say something to you,
I'd say listen to your heart, do something true.
But I know you will, 'cause you better than me.
You make me proud, Son,
hit that three.

70 – The Map

Martin's eyes misted over. "Thanks," he said.

"Of course," said Barrantine. "I hope you understand why I stopped off at your father's house. I sensed a misunderstanding there, as if parts were missing from the greater picture of your upbringing. Actually, Ana helped me grasp this. In the end, I felt no one should go through life without knowing he or she was loved."

Barrantine handed the second envelope to Martin. "With that, I'd like to introduce the final phase of our counseling. Please find the laminated piece of paper tucked inside. What you have in your hands is a map of a remote wilderness area outside of Winter Park. The map also corresponds to a certain set of mental categories I would like you to explore. What I would like for you to do in this final part of the counseling is to walk, both literally and figuratively, through certain places in nature, through certain places in your mind. I'd like you to experience total immersion, complete engagement. In short, I want your internal and external realities to converge, so there can be no escape."

Barrantine coughed. "So, to clarify, after your stay at my cabin, our counseling is complete. Our last official day as counselor and client will be when you leave the cabin. Too many times over the years, I've witnessed therapy sessions string on for too long, and there's a sense in which the therapy actually becomes part of the relationship. Everything becomes narrative, lots of talking; the counseling becomes routine, and couples lose sight of the true nature of change. I'd hate for that to happen here."

Martin put his arm around Ana.

"Here are the keys to the cabin. When you are done, please leave them in the coffee can outside. I recommend that you stay for at least three nights, and visit all of the key areas on the map. There are rooms inside the cabin. There are trails outside. There is a canyon leading to a lake on the property. I recall that you both like to hike and explore, to be active in mind and body, so please take this opportunity to seek out the paths of conscious and unconscious experience. And please consider the shadows on the walls of the cabin, as well as the boulders that have broken free from the cliff."

Barrantine stood up.

"I must now say goodbye. I wish you the best on your journey. And know that whatever happens, from the cabin and beyond, is going to be for the best. You are now at a place where you can decide your future."

Tears streamed down Barrantine's face when he reached over and hugged Martin and Ana, holding it for several seconds while puddles formed on their backs.

71 –The Cabin

Ana read from a leather notebook while Martin followed a dirt road into the heart of the James Peak Wilderness. Passing by a pair of moose drinking from beaver ponds, they turned up a long, narrow driveway barely visible from the road. Barrantine had instructed them to park under a canopy of trees on the east side and cover their car with spruce bows. All aspects of the cabin were grounded in getting away from other human beings, from technology, from the demands of work, from anything that might distract from their relationship.

Martin unloaded the luggage and placed their backpacks near a stone fireplace in the main room of the cabin, labeled Room of Shadows. In front of the fireplace, a couch was angled toward an empty wall. Martin and Ana sat down for a few minutes, absorbed the quietness of the cabin, then placed a few items in their daypacks for a hike.

The temperature was a perfect 80 degrees when they began ascending the trail labeled Path of the Past. Ana read Barrantine's comments in the notebook, which suggested that they discuss their reasons for entering counseling, and that they do it in terms of their childhood. The notebook further stated that the discussion would be long and arduous just like the hike itself. Climbing a steep section of granite steps, Ana launched into talking about her parents.

"They never discussed their issues," she said. "They never argued. Everything was beneath the surface."

Martin understood more than Ana knew.

"When my father committed suicide," she continued, "it took away my confidence. I became scared of the future and I needed security. I still have these fears. When there is conflict at my job, I feel a slight loss of control, the future less certain. I think I obsess about work. And with my dad losing his job before he died, there's also that."

Ana turned to Martin, fell into his arms. "God, I miss him," she said, her body shaking. "I really miss him. My dad was so smart, so kind. I just don't know what happened. I don't know what went wrong in his life. I guess it was the depression."

Martin looked up at the clouds. "Life is really hard," he said, rubbing Ana's back. "Sometimes I wonder why more people don't come to this conclusion. I honestly think your dad was unlucky—unlucky to have the outlook he did. You know what I mean? He didn't choose darkness. It chose him. I just wish I could have met him."

"I do, too. You would have really liked my dad. He was easy going in a lot of ways, non-judgmental. He would have loved you, too."

Ana and Martin continued along the Path of the Past. Now 2:00 in the afternoon, a diaphanous layer of clouds covered the sun. They hit tree line at 10,000 feet. The air was light, trees sparse, rocks had a razor-sharp quality. The surrounding peaks seemed imbued with personality, full of dialogue, in concert with the glaciers, the sky, the trees, the purple Columbine flowers. Everything felt like something else.

"Martin, my mom and dad had a bad relationship."

"Bad? What do you mean?"

"I was idealizing it," she said. "Really, I was. My parents had communication issues, major ones. And I denied it. I denied it because of how they portrayed themselves. The truth is, my parents were actors, and I bought into their roles. It wasn't real. Martin, I don't ever want us to be like them. I don't want to pretend. I want us to be able to talk, to have open lines of communication."

Now descending the other side of the mountain, they began the approach to the Glacier of Commitment and Boulders Where We Fall. Along the way, they followed a series of switchbacks and crossed an alpine meadow until they arrived at a platform of metamorphosed gneiss, where Barrantine had etched his signature at the base of the platform and wrote Bench of Anger. They sat down.

Ana looked across the valley to the enormous boulder field.

"Martin, I was with another man," she said, her voice flat. "I mean, after our separation."

Martin withdrew his hand from Ana's thigh. "What?"

"I realize I messed up badly." Ana's words pinged off the boulders. "But it made me understand you. It made me want you more."

"Want me? What do you want in me? All I seem to do is make your life more difficult."

"That's not true."

Martin crossed his arms. "Why? Why did you do it? To get back at me?"

"No," said Ana. "It was just a confusing night. I'd been drinking, and I was in a bad headspace after what happened."

"Who were you with? Did you know him beforehand?"

"He was a stranger."

"Was he a white guy? Did you sleep with him?"

"No, he wasn't a white guy," said Ana biting her lip. "Yes, I did sleep with him, and it felt horrible and icky."

The wind blew through the canyon. Leaves, small branches twirled through the air.

"Why would it matter if he was white?"

Martin pulled on his ear. "It matters because maybe you want someone else?"

"Oh, please. All I've ever wanted is you."

"And your mom? How does she feel about our relationship?"

"Martin, I have no idea where this is coming from. My mom loves you. She doesn't care about stuff like that." Ana placed her fingers on Martin's chin and turned his face toward her. "And who was the woman who you were with? What was her ethnicity?"

"She was brown, Latina."

"Great, and how do you think that makes me feel?"

"I don't know."

"How about inadequate."

Martin stood up, examined the entire expanse of the Boulders Where We Fall, which seemed endless, inhospitable. Only a marmot scampering around gave the rocks life. "You're right," he said. "I'm sure it feels very demeaning. I'm sorry. I'm so sorry. It was stupid…and totally meaningless."

He sat back down, wrapped his arms around Ana, while the wind blew through her hair, and boulders started to crumble, dislodge, tumble down the bowl below. The sound was guttural, like the earth had coughed up rocks from its core. The mountain shook. Electricity permeated the air; maybe a dry storm was on the way. Martin felt the coolness of Ana's body. He felt his thoughts turn inward, toward the boundless landscape inside himself.

Martin's frontal lobe started to warm. His limbic system began to roil. The region of his brain that was responsible for distributing commitment and carnality in equal measure across his cortex began to move in waves. Subtle configurations of grey matter formed along his cerebellum, along the Weather Region of his brain. And when he looked out across the boulder field to the mountains in the distance, the sun had fallen, the rocks and trees disappeared. The sky grew dark.

72 – Taming Banshee

Desmond, Zeke and Nate ducked into a cave. Hungry from the swim, Desmond offered Nate a tin of sardines, which Nate socked back ravenously, thanking them for the meal. Trust started to build between the cells. Eventually, Desmond broke out the vodka and the conversation started flowing. Desmond and Zeke started talking mermaids, why the luscious creatures drove them crazy, what it was about their bodies that made their loins tingle. Nate started talking philosophy, particularly ethics and God. The concepts were way out of Desmond and Zeke's wheelhouse, but started to gain purchase when Nate brought up Chuck.

"So, let me try to understand this a little better. Before you had relations with this ambiguous mermaid, you hurt your leader, Chuck?"

Desmond looked down.

"Yeah, Chuck passed."

"Now, in my world," said Nate, "this would represent a very serious moral wrong. It would be wrong to kill your leader in order to have sex with a mermaid, even if said mermaid was really attractive."

Desmond twitched slightly. "I think I get it."

Nate looked at his oxygen levels. "So I think it's fair to say that this sneaky mermaid has turned vengeful and sadistic. Here's what my dad taught me about this kind of stuff. In order to not be overwhelmed by these forces, you have to change the trajectory of the sin. You have to outwit the devil, indirectly."

"Outwit the devil? Indirectly?" asked Zeke.

"Yes, or in your idiom, trick this bitch. My dad always told me that sin must be distracted and changed in a covert way."

"You sayin' we trick this ho with morality in a funny sort of way?" queried Zeke.

"Right, you can't battle sin head-on. It's too powerful. Don't forget those sharp fingernails and razor-like teeth. So, we have to have a strategy, right? I'm thinking that morality might work, as in we lay a couple moral precepts on her and see how she reacts."

"Moral precepts?" said Desmond.

"Yes, as in rules about how you ought to act in relation to God." Nate was trying to keep it simple. "So, given that everyone here in the Sea seems pretty into sensory pleasures, I'm thinking music might be not be a bad option, as in really bad choral music to make her feel a sense of guilt."

"Guilt?"

"Yes, guilt, via the moral precepts, which is how it usually goes when cells feel guilt. Now, I don't know if this will work, but it's worth a try. Who knows, she might actually have sympathy for moral matters."

"Really?" said Desmond. "You really think this might work?"

"Really," affirmed Nate. "Trust me when I say that morality has a major impact on creatures. Like it can cause entire groups to fall under its spell. Cells will do all kinds of things under its power. Some good, some bad."

"Bad morality?"

"Yep, sounds like an oxymoron, but it's true—bad morality. It's actually pretty common."

"Interesting," said Desmond.

"All right, so let's shore up our plan. First, we heap a heavy dose of morality on Banshee via the choral music, hoping she will experience guilt."

"Got that," said Desmond.

"Then, if she takes the guilt bait, I say we lead her back here to the cave." Nate shined his flashlight on the walls. "Music might not be enough, right? So, I'm thinking we need to add another layer. I say we do a show for her, a little morality play so to speak, on the walls of the cave, using shadows and the like." Nate looked at his regulator. "My oxygen is getting low. I gotta go. Does this sound like a plan?"

Desmond and Zeke nodded briskly.

73 – Bench of Anger

Martin and Ana had fallen asleep on the Bench of Anger. When they awoke, eight hours had passed, and a layer of frost had formed over the boulder field below. They sat up and scanned the valley. Low-hanging clouds with puffy purple centers hovered over the trees. A slight wind blew through the canyon. A golden eagle flew overhead. The mountain seemed cautious, ready to talk. But would they be able to listen?

Martin held Ana's hand as they traversed the top of the boulder field where shards of rock had compacted to form a faint trail. A light rain started to come down, the kind of precipitation aimed only at them, one hundred drops of water, a sky of full of intentionality.

"When it started raining in April," said Martin, "when you left for your conference, I started drinking before I went to Barrantine's. I felt stressed, like I needed to let go. Ana, there are times when I feel like I want to get away from it all. Not from life, but the routine, all the shit we have to do in our lives."

Ana listened in silence.

"I guess I feel like a complicated person. Like I'm really not simple at all. And it tires me out. It really does. And I just want to get away, lose myself. But then life gets even more complicated because when I get in that my mindset, I'm susceptible to making bad decisions."

"Is this how you felt when I left for the conference?"

"Pretty much. You know the story about my stepdad cutting out the crotches of my mom's underwear?"

"Yes."

"We discussed that."

"What else was said?"

"A lot. My dad was a big one. I guess I've been angry at him for a long time, and it turns out, maybe I was wrong about some of it. You know, I just wanted to escape the situation with my mom. I *needed* to escape. I hated living with her. She was crazy, man. Crazy. I probably sound like a broken record, but she's got some real mental illness going on, and I didn't want to be around her. And I damn sure didn't want to be like her. But then I also see a little of herself in me, which I hate."

"What do you hate?"

Martin shook his head. "Probably all the damn emotion. Like right now. I feel like I've got all these strong, crazy, irrational feelings swirling around."

"I understand," said Ana, "but you need to remember that emotion is good. It's what makes you, you. It's also what makes your food taste good."

"I'm not so sure. Might be more of my dad's influence."

Martin and Ana now stood at the top of the Glacier of Commitment, where a blue rubble river had pooled and froze to form the great monolith. Ana put on a pair of sunglasses. The glare from the glacier was strong.

"Can I ask you a question?" she said, her eyes scanning the dirt and rocks embedded in the glacier.

"Yes."

"Was this the first time you were with another woman?"

Martin was quiet for several seconds. "I've crossed a couple lines before, but never like that."

Ana's shoulders tightened. Her face reddened. Her mouth seized up. Panic took hold, like she wanted to get away from the glacier, escape its hidden crevasses. Maybe it was unstable, too dangerous to even be around?

Martin put his arm around Ana and led her down the trail, away from the glacier. Eventually, they descended to the valley floor and followed a creek that weaved through bushes and trees, tucking under rocks, widening as it flowed down the basin. Feeling more relaxed, Ana read from the notebook, where Barrantine spoke about the importance of pondering the connection between Channel Creek and the Glacier of Commitment. He also mentioned the possibility of finding wild raspberries scattered throughout the valley. Sure enough, hundreds of the dime-sized fruit were right at their feet. They leaned over, grabbed a handful of berries and continued their trek through the valley.

Martin started talking about his new job.

"It's early, but I feel like the food truck has been good for me. I needed to find a new outlet. I realize it's less secure, and the money is not quite there yet, but I had all this bad energy from my last job. I don't know, I feel like it will help me stay more balanced, and eventually, the food truck should be pretty profitable."

Ana had pangs of uncertainty, which she hated in herself. Could Martin pay the bills on a food truck salary? Would his eyes wander around drunken women? Would he get drunk himself?

"I'm happy for you, babe. I think you needed a change of pace. I'm sure your food truck is going to be a smashing success."

"Thanks."

"So, I was thinking about something as well," said Ana.

"What's that?"

"Would you consider taking dance lessons with me? I know it's not really your cup of tea, but it might be fun, and I feel like it would be good for us. We could do salsa, or hip hop, or whatever. It just would give us a new activity to help break up the routine. We could probably find dance lessons on Friday nights. Maybe we could do happy hour first, then dance."

Martin's head swerved in a figure eight motion. "We can do that."

Ana smiled. "Look," she said, pointing to a break in the trees. "The trail is starting to widen." She studied the map. "Surface Lake."

Sure enough, they had arrived at the edge of a meadow and could see Channel Creek snake back-and-forth. In the distance, the sun glistened off the water. The aroma of wildflowers hit their noses. Martin and Ana took off their shoes and began walking through the meadow, crossing the creek several times, on their way to the final landmark of their ten-mile journey.

74 – Mountain Counseling

When they arrived at Surface Lake, the wind was calm. A small herd of white-tailed deer ate grass in the distance. Martin laid out a blanket for Ana. She sat down, felt her thoughts wander, push inward, as if she had missed something in Barrantine's mountain counseling. Maybe she hadn't paid close enough attention to the trail. Perhaps there was a feature of the canyon she did not fully explore. Although she remembered Barrantine using the word "surface" or "surfacing" a time or two in their sessions, she couldn't recall exactly what it meant. As usual, his methods seemed powerful, transcendent, beyond the instructions in the map and notebook.

Ana looked to the far side of the meadow where the grass grew tall. She listened to the sound of rainbow trout sipping caddis flies on the lake. Ana drew a mental picture of her father who loved to fish. If only he would have visited *this* meadow, she thought, things would be different. She would be different. If only he could have walked along the creek and spent time at the life-sustaining glacier. If only he could have explored the network of trails and let their branches take him to places unknown. What would it have been like, she wondered, if her father were looking up at these snow-capped peaks? What if her father were here right now?

Wind blew through Ana's hair.

A meadowlark sang as it flew over Surface Lake.

An hour passed. Martin came back from a walk to the edge of the meadow. The sun was fading over the mountaintops. The air grew cold. They could see each other's breath. Martin turned on his headlamp. "I guess it's time to go back," he said, "time to finish the loop."

"Yes, time to finish the loop," said Ana, glancing at the map. "Looks like a pretty short hike back."

"Sounds good. Should we hit it? I'm hungry."

"Me too."

The hike back to the cabin took a half hour. When they arrived, Martin placed pine needles in his pockets and grabbed a handful of kindling from the woodshed. Upon entering, he launched into making a fire in the Room of Shadows. True to its name, flames blazed through the tempered glass, projecting dark figures on the empty wall of the cabin.

Ana lay on the couch, wrapped herself in a blanket and felt the motions of Martin's penumbra move across the wall while he rummaged through cabinets looking for what to cook for dinner. As the fire crackled, Ana recalled her dream on the Fourth of July. The one where the witch-like figure rode the mustang on the beach, slowly sinking in the depths of the sea, her fiery eyes staring back at Ana hiding on the hillside.

Martin found a tortilla press, avocados, tomatoes, rice, cilantro, onions. Although there was nothing specific written in the notebook, by all appearances, Barrantine had planned for him to show off his food truck recipes. Martin followed his lead, slicing onions, radishes and a jalapeno, his shadow bending and twisting as garlic simmered over the gas stove. Ana stood up, placed a log on the fire, poured herself a glass of red wine and tried to fall into the darkest part of the shadows.

"So, what have your mom and dad been up to the last few months?" she asked. "Have you talked to them?"

Martin set down the knife. "No, I haven't talked to my mom for ages. And, my dad, I spoke to him briefly after he got out of the hospital. I did mention our separation, though. He was sad. Said you're a good one and I should fight for you."

Ana smiled. "That's sweet. I think we should invite Alonzo

over soon. It would be good to reconnect—for both of us, even. It's funny because even though our dads are so different, seeing Alonzo used to make me feel closer to my own dad in ways. And with his health not being good, I think it's important to reconnect...before it is too late. Trust me, you don't want to cross that threshold without a proper goodbye."

Martin walked around the corner. "I guess we can invite him over sometime," he said, leaning over to kiss Ana out of the side of his mouth. "Check it out, our shadows are kissing."

Charmed, Ana grabbed Martin and pulled him to the couch.

"Now they're hugging."

Martin lay across Ana's lap.

"Speaking of shadows, did Barrantine ever discuss yours?"

Ana considered many things at once. "A little bit, I guess. At one point, he compared me to a house whose windows and doors were shut," she said, laughing.

"Oh, really. Why don't you tell me about this house," said Martin.

"Only after you tell me more about your shadow."

75 – Morality Under the Sea

Time was short. Nate would need to swim hard to reach the island before Banshee had consumed the sperm whale. Thankfully, the tide was coming in, and a longshore current whipped him to shore. Once on shore, he unzipped his backpack and fished for the last of his items. A deck of playing cards. A candle. His music player. A mixtape his father had made him years ago. The A-side had some Dylan, Cash and Coltrane; the B-side some old choral music by the Angel Neuron Tabernacle.

Nate contemplated which side to play. Concerned that the greatness of Dylan, Cash and Coltrane might actually undermine the message, Nate flipped to the B-side and listened to the first song. *Ewww, that's bad.* Nate felt torn by the decision. Should he start Banshee off with Trane, then move to the other stuff? *Yep, makes sense.* He placed the rest of his gear in his dive pack, hooked up new oxygen tanks and prepared to make the trip back to the cave.

Now more familiar with entering the Sea, he stepped onto the rocks and slipped into the water with ease, this time making it past the breakers and turning the corner within minutes. Nate dove down deep and within an hour had arrived at the cave.

Desmond was eagerly waiting at the entrance. "Great, you're here."

"Yes, definitely, are you ready?" Nate extracted the waterproof tape player from his dive pack.

"Roger that," said Desmond, handing Nate the sea megaphone.

Nate, Desmond and Zeke started swimming toward Banshee. When they reached the edge of the blood halo, they knew it was time to begin. Nate held up the megaphone and hit play on Coltrane's "A Love Supreme, Pt I." Banshee, who was scraping whale fat from her upper lip, looked up. *What the fuck?* she said to herself quietly. Banshee began to follow the harmonic dissonance of Trane.

The Diver Neurons could immediately recognize the nasty witch was off-kilter.

"I think it is working," said Desmond.

"Keep dat shit going, mane," said Zeke.

Nate turned up the volume. "A Love Supreme, Pt. 1" ended. Dylan was next. Interestingly, Pastor Samuel chose "Ye Shall Be Changed" off Dylan's *The Bootleg Series, Volume 3*. Banshee now listened to the words, which sent her to a new level of introspection when Dylan sung about surrendering to God. She kept swimming, following the music, which grew increasingly layered with moral content, as it moved through Cash's "I Came to Believe" off *American V: A Hundred Highways*, recorded during the last year of his life. Banshee's mind moved to a place it never had before and started to soften.

Although Zeke and Desmond were likewise taken in by the metaphysical qualities of the music, it was time to lay it on thick.

Nate flipped the tape over and hit play on the Angel Neuron Tabernacle. The musical mood changed. Overt and straightforward words of forgiveness and repentance for your sins traveled on the backs of the music molecules to Banshee, who, now visibly irritated, placed her wrinkled hands over her deformed ears. Despite herself, she began to follow the music toward its source. Five songs later, she had reached the cave. Nate, Zeke and Desmond were huddled behind a rock.

"Damn, this shit is wack," whispered Zeke to Nate. "I mean, not the early stuff. I'm talking these last few songs."

"I hear you," said Nate, extracting his underwater flashlight from his side pocket. "But the plan is working. We hooked her with a few timeless classics, then buttered her up with church stuff. Now it's time for the final act. You remember the plan, right?"

"Sure," said Zeke, placing his index dendrite in front of the flashlight, creating the shadow of a sperm whale on the wall of the cave. But just as the show was about to start, the battery on the tape player went south, and the songs slowed down, became incomprehensible.

"The hell with it," said Nate to Zeke. "I'll have to take this one home myself."

Nate placed the megaphone to his mouth and started singing hymns he knew by heart. Funny enough, the live aspect of the music, along with its unsophisticated moral content, actually frazzled Banshee even more; her eyes were nearly closed, mouth sucked in.

Desmond edged over and readied his character. Using four dendrites, he skillfully conjured up the shadow of a full set of cock and balls on the walls of the cave. Then he proceeded to portray the cock and balls as penetrating the sperm whale in a sexual manner, which made Banshee become downright contemplative. Banshee started to ponder the causal connections between her own sexual escapades and the attack of the sperm whale.

"Yes," said Nate, in between verses. "Perfect."

Nate gestured for Desmond to incorporate the religious symbolism into the play. Desmond responded by making a shadow of a Christian cross floating above the cock and balls. Zeke followed suit by making a new shadow puppet with his free dendrite. The image of a Devil with horns, which Nate hadn't even instructed him to do, danced on the wall.

"Hell yes," said Nate under his breath in between lines about Satan, "Hell, yes!"

At this point, having been thoroughly matrixed by guilt, Banshee's mind turned to a pile of mush. Not a peep of any kind left her dirty little mouth. Not a squeal, not a howl. In short, Banshee had been pummeled by what Nate regarded as a kind of pedestrian morality, and Banshee regretted each and every one of her actions—corrupting the Sea, damaging ear drums, wiping out libidos, transmitting sexual diseases, driving mermaids to God knows where, all of it. Banshee's entire essence began to fold back in on itself, including her very own body, which morphed back into its original transexual state.

"Sorry," Banshee whispered in a meek voice. "I'm sorry for pretending to be what I was not."

Several million Diver Neurons nodded. Many thought Banshee looked doable again, and their loins started to tingle. Strange how things can change so quickly.

"And what *were* you?" asked Nate.

Desmond nudged Nate. "Let's not go there. Let's let bygones be bygones."

"I'm just a sea creature like yourselves," said Banshee. "But I often feel lost and lonely, a little unaccepted, because the Sea feels endless, and there are not a lot of mermaids like me. I'm a minority figure, basically."

Where had this Banshee been? Desmond and Zeke wondered to themselves.

Nate swam over to Banshee and put his arm around her. "Oh, I'm sure there are many mermaids like you. I'd say give it time. And don't worry about what others think. They'll evolve."

Suddenly, an object passed by the entrance of the cave, and a wave rolled in, throwing a good many Diver Neurons into the limestone. Thankfully, no one was injured. Desmond shined his light into the distance. "Is that what I think it is?"

"Huh?" said Zeke, with a look of shock.

The sperm whale peered into the cave.

"Hello," it said, in a soft voice.

"You still alive?" asked Zeke.

"I'm a little hurt," the sperm whale responded. "Actually, I'm a lot hurt, and I'm still tending to my wounds. But, at this point, the majority of my pain is emotional."

Banshee was hiding behind a rock. A group of Diver Neurons nudged her forward. "Ummm...I wasn't aware that you can talk," she said, her voice cracking.

The sperm whale nodded its head. "I just learned English, actually. I thought it was necessary...to make peace with you."

Banshee's eyes grew wide. Her words were stuck in her throat. "Yeah, ummm...I'm super sorry for what I did there earlier, for attacking you and such. I'm not sure what came over me."

"I understand. We all make mistakes." The sperm whale rested its lower jaw on the cave entrance. "I overheard your earlier comments about being different. I am the largest toothed creature in the Sea. I know what it feels like to be different."

Zeke, Desmond and the rest of the Diver Neurons wore blank expressions.

The sperm whale gestured with its small flippers for Banshee to come closer. "Should we take this conversation elsewhere?"

"Ummm...we can do that."

"Shall we go then?"

"Sure," said Banshee, following the sperm whale out of the cave.

Meanwhile, Desmond lined up shots of tequila.

"Can you f'n believe it?" said Desmond.

"Nah, man, are you kidding me?" said Zeke. "That shit was

off the charts. A mermaid who turned into witch, then back into a mermaid...a talking sperm whale." Zeke placed his dendrite on Nate's shoulder. "A fellow neuron brotha who came from the Sky. Woo! Now, that's some crazy shit."

The two Diver Neurons slapped five. "Cheers."

"Hey," said Zeke, looking at Desmond. "While we're on the subject, I have something I want to tell you, something I've been thinking 'bout for a while now."

"Let her rip, tater chip," said Desmond.

"I fucked up there, man—big time."

"Fucked up? What do you mean?" asked Desmond.

"I mean, in the past with Chuck. I'm sorry about Chuck, man. He was a good dude, and I did him wrong, very wrong. Same goes for you. I did you real wrong. I'm sorry for blindsiding you with the punch and for calling you a bitch." Zeke pursed his lips and twisted a dreadlock. "You know what, I don't deserve to be the leader of us no more. You the leader, Dez. You the leader now."

Zeke and Desmond embraced in a full-on nucleus-to-nucleus hug.

"Thanks," replied Desmond, "I accept your apology. And I know Chuck would be happy to see how far you've come since you first joined the expedition. And he would acknowledge that everyone makes mistakes. The way I see it is, shit happens. You live and learn. Then you move on, we move on—on to tracking new mermaid cooch."

They laughed, turned toward Nate.

"Nate, we'd like thank you for what you did for us," said Desmond. "But how can we ever repay you? I don't really ever think we'll be able to make a trip up there to the Sky."

Nate shook his head. "No need for repayment, guys. You're the ones I'd like to thank."

"For what?" asked Zeke.

Nate became philosophical. "For giving me an opportunity to realize my potential," he said. "I've been looking for greater meaning in my life, to be fully engaged with what matters, to make a difference, you know. But I wasn't sure how to go about it. Church sure as hell wasn't doing it for me. Neither was the Sky. I guess I always felt like there was more to experience, and I never totally believed in the horror stories about the Sea. Turns out the Sea is actually a pretty cool place. Complicated and a little dangerous, but cool."

Desmond and Zeke squinted.

Nate looked up. "And the other thing...this gave me the chance to make my dad proud. What's funny is my dad was totally against my decision. Everyone was. But I know he would be proud of me now. I know he would think this is pretty cool. My dad is all about helping your neighbor and trying to make the world a better place." Nate's lip quivered. He looked at his regulator. "Well, guys, my oxygen is low, and this is my last canister. Time for me to head back. Hey, what do you say we do one before I leave?"

Desmond poured three shots of Patron. The neurons clinked glasses, tossed back the shots of tequila, no chaser. "Goodbye," said Nate, swimming up to the light at the surface of the Sea. "Maybe I'll catch you again someday. Hopefully, this isn't the last time we cross paths."

76 – Confirmation

Today was the final day at the cabin. Martin and Ana were heading back to Denver later that afternoon. A sense of uncertainty, a cautious feeling, hung in the air as they packed up their belongings and wondered what the last three days meant. Yes, the counseling was effective, but could they really trust their feelings? Had Martin really channeled his impulses in the right way? Had Ana dealt with her father's death, so she could be the kind of person she wanted for herself and Martin?

Ana could hear Barrantine's rounded voice when she read from the last page of the notebook:

"The final day of counseling should be dedicated to establishing continuity, to shoring up insights, to asking lingering questions. It's true the last three days might not feel real. Perhaps your entire life doesn't feel real. But all of this is normal—loose ends, that is, unsettled feelings, doubts about where you have been and what it means to move forward. Whatever you have decided, it is important for you to verify your feelings, make sure they have true staying power and are conducive to a secure future. And that is the focal point of day four."

Taking a walk back to Surface Lake, a nervous energy pervaded the forest while they searched for a final clue to crystalize their experiences from the last three days. Nothing was off limits. The entire natural world was open to interpretation— the shape of the trees, the expressions of the rocks, the types of plants along the trail, the direction of the wind. Yet, when they set their backpacks down on the bank of Surface Lake, they were at a loss. Only a vague sense of doubt seemed to drift from the steam on the lake.

Ana put on sunglasses and looked in the direction of the

sun.

"Well, we both have to work tomorrow. Maybe we should try to beat the traffic. Do you think we should leave?"

Leave. The word felt hollow. Neither of them wanted to leave. They each wanted to find a reason to stay. But what was the reason? What did Barrantine want them to discover on the final day?

At a loss for words, Martin fumbled around in his backpack, pulled out a felt bag.

"What's that?" asked Ana.

"A watch."

Ana blinked slowly. "Oh, the One-Sentence watch."

"No, this one is different. I forgot to give it back to Barrantine."

"What does it do?"

Martin held it in the air. "It's like the other watch, but instead of erasing words, it erases impulses or desires, or sort of resets them anyway. I know we are supposed to be getting away from technology, but should we try it, just for fun? Maybe it will give us new impulses, or confirm which ones really matter."

Ana placed the watch on her wrist. "Sure. Tell me when you are ready."

"I'm ready. So, where do we go from here?" asked Martin.

"Here? I don't know."

Martin gestured for Ana to push the button. "So, where do we go from here?" he said again.

Ana pushed the button.

"Maybe we should go for a swim?!"

Martin's eyebrows lifted. "A swim? Sure, sounds good to me."

"But I didn't bring a bathing suit," said Ana.

This time Ana pushed the button on the One-Impulse Time Machine watch with no prodding. A strong impulse entered her mind. "I guess we will have to go nude," she said, taking off her clothes.

Martin scanned Ana's naked body. She was shaved. Everywhere. Wow, he said to himself silently. They jumped in the water.

"Burrr, it's cold."

Martin swam over, ran his hands along her shoulders and hips, moved to her backside, cupped her from behind. He touched her breasts, slid down her stomach to her shavedness. Although she squirmed slightly, Ana was less restrained than usual.

"Well, I'm definitely awake now, but I'm thinking we should get out," she said. "I don't think I can fully relax in this cold water."

They dried off. Martin straightened a towel, helped Ana to her back. They kissed slowly. Martin massaged Ana's shoulders, then her sides. He spread her legs apart. Ana commented on the One-Impulse Time Machine. "Maybe I should use it while we're having sex?" The thought turned Martin on, and he pushed himself inside. But Ana wasn't joking. She reached above her head, reattached the watch and hit the button.

"Yes!" she screamed out, as Martin thrust into her.

Ana pushed the button again, and the same scream left her mouth, only this time she wrapped her legs around Martin so that he could hardly move.

His sexual hackles on high alert, Martin tried to resist Ana's force, moving in and out in short, quick motions. But the intensity of the lovemaking overwhelmed him, and he could only last for another ninety seconds. He rolled over, exhausted. "Ummm, that was really good. I guess I'm a little out of practice."

Ana giggled. "All right, but you better be ready for round two here soon!"

"Yes, give me a minute."

Ana took the One-Impulse Time Machine watch off her wrist, handed it to Martin. "Here, your turn."

"My turn, okay. When do you want me to push it?"

"Whenever you are ready," said Ana. "Actually, let me ask you a question. Do you think the counseling and everything we've been through these last few months really made a difference?"

"Yes," said Martin.

Ana gestured for him to push the button, which he did.

"Yes," he said again.

"How so?" she asked.

"I think I've found new meaning in my life."

"Meaning?" said Ana.

"Yes, meaning...meaning that our relationship feels like something greater."

They laughed at the play on words.

"Tell me more," said Ana.

"It's kind of hard to explain. I guess it feels like when I am with you, I am breaking free from my past. Like, you are what my mother is not. And, we, as a couple, are everything my parents were not. We make each other better, or at least you make me better. And that's the greatest complement I could ever give to another person—you make my life more meaningful. You help me strive to be my better self."

"Wow, that's really sweet," said Ana. "And deep."

"What about you?" asked Martin. "Do you think the counseling made a difference?"

"Well, I definitely can't put it as eloquently as you did, but yes, I do."

"How so?"

"Oh, I'd echo what you said. I guess I understand myself a little more. And I feel like it made me appreciate why we chose each other in the first place. Martin, I cherish our differences, and I love how you push me out of my comfort zone. It makes me thankful." Ana put her hair in a ponytail. "I do have a question for you, though."

"Yes."

"I love what you said today. I mean, it melted my heart. But can you trust your feelings over the long term?"

"Definitely."

"How do you know?" asked Ana.

"How do I know? Because of what we have built together. Because of the counseling. Because of where this has led us. To the dancing on the Friday nights. To my new job. To reconnecting with my father. To possibly even building a stronger relationship with your mother."

"I'd love that," said Ana, tilting her head to the side. "I've just never seen this side of you. I've never seen you so communicative in this way."

Martin shrugged his shoulders. "I hear you. It is different. I guess I feel like I've broken through some sort of mental barrier. Probably sounds a little hokey."

"No, it doesn't sound hokey at all. Tell me more."

"I'm not sure there's much more I can say, other than I feel like we needed to go through these struggles, or I needed it, anyway. I'm not trying to justify what happened, but maybe the last few months were necessary—all the pain and misery, I mean."

Ana ran her hands down Martin's arm. "Okay, I think I can accept that a certain amount of misery was necessary, but going forward, can we not put ourselves through the whole problem of evil thing again?"

Martin smirked. "You remembered?"

"How could I forget? It's all you talked about that semester." Ana looked at her watch. "It's 3:00. Do you think we should consider heading home?"

Martin started to loosen the One-Impulse Time Machine. "I guess so."

"Okay, but before you take the watch off, one last question," said Ana.

"Shoot."

"Are you really going to want me and only me ten years from now?"

"Yes, of course."

"Are you sure?" said Ana.

"Yes."

Ana smiled. "Really? Truly? Honestly?"

Martin pushed the button on the One-Impulse Time Machine.

77 – Pastor Samuel on Evil

It was late Sunday morning, and Pastor Samuel had just delivered a sermon on the union with God during troubling times. Although the congregation didn't notice, Pastor Samuel's sermon was flat and lacked conviction, the problem of evil having stripped him bare, leaving him in a great depression. How could a good God preside over the loss of a son? There was no answer to this question, no lesson here, no greater good. The theodicies didn't make a damn bit of sense. All that remained was darkness, the likes of which he had never experienced before.

With no interest in coffee and donuts, Pastor Samuel loosened his clerical collar, threw on a pair of cutoff shorts and walked to a place he had avoided for the last few months: his son's room. Pastor Samuel cautiously walked in, looked around. Adventure books were spread across Nate's bed, along with old philosophy paperbacks. Nietzsche's *Beyond Good and Evil* rested on top.

Pastor Samuel examined Nate's rock collection, his pens and pencils on the desk and the set of binoculars resting atop his record player. A sense of desperation took hold over as he wondered why Nate didn't take his binoculars. The thought sent him spiraling. He began to cry like a baby, the pain so intense he questioned his own ability to go on living without his son. The endless suffering ahead. The pretense of being strong. The false reality of a greater good, that any of this made even a shred of cosmic sense. For a minute, Pastor Samuel reflected on eastern philosophy, on the Samurai code of seppuku, more specifically, of taking one's own life in the face of the enemy.

Walking into the kitchen where Nate had cut the hole in

Jake Camp is a writer and philosophy professor who lives in Arvada, CO with his sons. His first novel, *Facticity Blues*, was published in 2016. Please check out his website: www.jake-camp.com

Pski's Porch Publishing was formed July 2012, to make books for people who like people who like books. We hope we have some small successes. **www.pskisporch.com.**

Pski's Porch

323 East Avenue
Lockport, NY 14094
www.pskisporch.com

Made in USA - Crawfordsville, IN
50044_9781948920148
05.13.2021 2003